This Walker book belongs to:

_____

_____

_____

First published 2014 by Walker Books Ltd, 87 Vauxhall Walk, London SE11 5HJ

This edition published 2015

Illustrations first published in *Mr. William Shakespeare's Plays* (1998)
and *Bravo, Mr. William Shakespeare!* (2000)

2 4 6 8 10 9 7 5 3 1

This book has been typeset in Truesdell and Centaur

Printed in China

British Library Cataloguing in Publication Data: a catalogue record for
this book is available from the British Library

ISBN 978-1-4063-6102-5

www.walker.co.uk

www.marciawilliams.co.uk

For Cora Belle
O wonderful, wonderful, and most wonderful
wonderful, and yet again wonderful,
and after that, out of all whooping!
— As You Like It

Tales from Shakespeare

As told by
Marcia Williams

WALKER BOOKS
AND SUBSIDIARIES
LONDON · BOSTON · SYDNEY · AUCKLAND

The Plays

Dear Playgoer,

Please take your seat and prepare to be transported to the world of Mr William Shakespeare! Yes, he was born 450 years ago, but trust me, he's the greatest. Shakespeare can still make your heart pound, skin crawl, eyes close tight in terror, legs collapse with laughter, and your hands clap until they are red raw.

Within these pages you will find characters of every shape and description, some of whom you may already know. They may come from Elizabethan England, but they could be living today. There is poor Bottom, the lovable fool — we all know a few of those — Macbeth and his wife, who will do anything for fame and glory, and Romeo and Juliet, so young and so in love, but caught up in a terrible family feud. Then there are creatures from another world, whom you may never meet again...

You will witness murders most foul, impossible love triangles, ghastly cruelty and amazing compassion — in other words, you will never be bored. So let the plays unfold. Imagine them however you want to, for Shakespeare wrote them for each and every one of us.

Marcia Williams

What a racket!

A Midsummer Night's Dream

The laws in ancient Athens were extremely harsh. One of the more outrageous laws decreed that a daughter must marry the man of her father's choice. If she chose to disobey her father, she risked having to live out her days in a nunnery – or, worse, forfeit her life. You would think that fathers would let their daughters choose their own husbands, but some of them would not. Take the grand Athenian gentleman Egeus, for example. He was a tyrant, and he had ordered his pretty, dark-eyed daughter Hermia to marry a noble called Demetrius. Demetrius was young, good looking and rich, and he loved Hermia – but Hermia did not love him. She loved his friend, Lysander, and Lysander loved her. The trouble was that Hermia's best friend, Helena, who was as tall and ungainly as Hermia was small and dainty, adored Demetrius with an all-consuming passion.

As a result of all this, not one of them was happy.

Hermia was as stubborn as her father and would not agree to marry Demetrius, so Egeus brought her to the court of Theseus, Duke of Athens. Surely the duke could persuade her to change her mind?

"Full of vexation come I, with complaint against my child," grumbled Egeus.

Hermia   Egeus   Theseus   Hippolyta   Lysander   Demetrius

"What say you, Hermia?" said the duke. "Be advised, fair maid, your father should be as a god!"

"I would my father look'd but with my eyes!" said Hermia.

Theseus was about to get married himself, so he was inclined to be sympathetic towards Hermia. He gave her four days to choose between love and duty. "Take time to pause," he gently advised her.

But love never pauses – it rushes on, untamed. Being in love himself, the duke should perhaps have realized this! Besides, those as headstrong and fiery as Hermia do not listen to advice, even from the Duke of Athens.

"O hell! To choose love by another's eyes!" Hermia grumbled to Lysander when they were alone. Unable to bear the thought of parting, Lysander and Hermia agreed to flee Athens and marry where Athenian law could not touch them. They confided their plan to no one except Helena. Hermia hoped the news that she was leaving and was about to marry Lysander would cheer Helena up – it would give her a chance to woo Demetrius! Poor Helena; she could not understand why Demetrius chose Hermia's scorn over her love.

"Take comfort: he no more shall see my face," Hermia told her friend. "Lysander and myself will fly this place. Farewell, sweet playfellow: pray thou for us. And good luck grant thee thy Demetrius!" She smiled and hugged her friend goodbye.

That night, while their family and friends slept, Hermia and Lysander fled to the woods, away from the city and its cruel law. Unfortunately Helena, hoping to gain Demetrius's attention, told him of Hermia and Lysander's flight. But her plan did not work. Demetrius was obsessed with Hermia and determined to get her back, so he set out after the runaway lovers. All the lovelorn Helena could do was to follow Demetrius, declaring her love every second of the way!

Once they reached the woods, Demetrius turned on Helena. "I love thee not, therefore pursue me not!" he cried, angrily.

Still she dogged his footsteps, so again he turned on her. "I tell you I do not nor I cannot love you!"

"And even for that do I love you the more," sniffed Helena. "I am your spaniel."

Try as he might, Demetrius could not shake her off. So the pair continued deeper and deeper into the woods, searching along every path for Lysander and Hermia.

Demetrius and Helena were so involved with their search that they didn't notice they were not the only ones in the wood that night.

In one glade, six Athenian workmen were secretly rehearsing a play for Duke Theseus's wedding to Hippolyta. If their play was chosen they would be richly rewarded, so they took the rehearsal seriously and were eager to entertain.

Most eager of all was Bottom the weaver, who thought he should play every part! "Let me play Thisby," he lisped. "I'll speak in a monstrous little voice. Let me play the lion too," he roared. "I will roar, that I will do any man's heart good to hear me!"

However, Peter Quince, who was directing the play, would only allow Bottom to play the lover, Pyramus. He made sure everyone got a part – he even had actors playing moonshine and a wall!

In another glade hid stranger folk than these. For the wood was the fairy kingdom of King Oberon and Queen Titania and their fairies, sprites, goblins and elves. The king and queen had recently quarrelled over a changeling boy that Queen Titania had stolen.

King Oberon wanted to have the boy for himself, but Titania would not let him go. So when Oberon came across his queen and her fairies that night he was not pleased.

"Ill met by moonlight, proud Titania," he grumbled darkly.

"What! Jealous Oberon!" returned Titania. "Fairies, skip hence: I have forsworn his bed and company."

Oberon decided to play a trick on Titania. He sent his naughty sprite, Puck, to find a plant called Love-in-idleness. If you put its juice on someone's eyes as they slept, they would love the first creature they saw upon waking.

Puck's eyes glinted with delight. There was nothing he loved more than tricks and trouble! "I'll put a girdle round about the earth in forty minutes!" he cried as he vanished into the night.

Now, as it happened, Demetrius and Helena passed close to where Oberon sat waiting for Puck's return. Oberon could not help overhearing what passed between the pair.

"I am sick when I do look on thee," Demetrius shouted at Helena.

"And I am sick when I look not on you," she sniffed.

Then off they went again, Demetrius chasing Hermia, and Helena chasing Demetrius!

Oberon was touched by Helena's devotion, which was so unlike his own queen's, and he decided that she should have Demetrius. So, when Puck returned, Oberon told him to wait until the couple slept and then anoint Demetrius's eyelids with the juice of the magic

plant. Demetrius would then wake to see Helena, and love her for ever more.

"Thou shalt know the man by the Athenian garments he hath on," Oberon said.

"Fear not, my lord, your servant shall do so," cried Puck, vanishing in an instant.

Meanwhile, Oberon had his own plan. He set out in search of his sleeping queen. When he found her, he squeezed the flower's magic juice upon her eyelids.

"What thou seest, when thou dost wake, do it for thy true-love take, be it ounce, or cat, or bear. Wake when some vile thing is near," he whispered in Titania's ear. Then he vanished into the shadows to wait and watch.

Puck was also busy anointing a pair of eyes with the flower's juice. "Weeds of Athens he doth wear: this is he, my master said," he thought. Only unfortunately it was the wrong "he"! Puck had mistaken Lysander for Demetrius and had put the flower's juice on his eyes as he lay sleeping close to Hermia. And then, as luck would have it, Helena, still in pursuit of Demetrius, tripped over Lysander in the dark and woke him. So Lysander instantly forgot his love for Hermia and fell in love with Helena!

"Not Hermia, but Helena I love," he cried.

"Do not say so," exclaimed Helena. "Wherefore was I to this keen mockery born?"

Shocked and confused by Lysander's unexpected declaration of love, Helena ran off. Lysander followed close on her heels, crying, "To honour Helen, and to be her knight!"

Thus poor Hermia woke alone. "Lysander! Alack, where are you? I swoon almost with fear," she cried. Terrified, she set out in search of her beloved Lysander.

All this while Titania slept on, unaware that the troupe of Athenians, led by Bottom and Peter Quince, had chosen to rehearse their play in a nearby glade.

"Speak, Pyramus – Thisby, stand forth," Peter Quince ordered his actors.

It was the perfect opportunity for Puck to play one of his tricks, for Titania's eyelids still glistened with magic juice and he wanted to make sure she fell in love with something truly vile when she awoke. So he cast a spell on Bottom the weaver. Suddenly, in the middle of the play, Bottom came out from behind a bush with his head turned into a hairy ass's head!

"O monstrous!" shouted Peter Quince. "O strange! We are haunted. Pray masters, fly!"

The other actors fled in fright. Puck guided Bottom by magic to the sleeping Titania's side. There he left him, and retired to watch events unfold

Poor Bottom didn't realize he had been transformed. He thought his friends were making fun of him. "I see their knavery," he said. "This is to make an ass of me, to fright me if they could. I will sing, that all shall hear I am not afraid." But he was quaking with fear!

"The ousel-cock, so black of hue,

With orange-tawny bill,

The throstle with his note so true,

The wren with little quill," sang Bottom, with an ass's bray.

"What angel wakes me from my flowery bed?" cried Titania, woken by the sound. When she saw Bottom, she instantly fell in love with him, even though he had an ass's head!

Bottom was not displeased by the queen's attention, especially when she ordered her fairies to attend his every whim.

"Peaseblossom! Cobweb! Moth! And Mustardseed! Be kind and courteous to this gentleman; hop in his walks, and gambol in his eyes; feed him with apricocks and dewberries," she cried.

Puck reported all this to the delighted Oberon. As they were talking, Demetrius and Hermia paused close by.

"Stand close," whispered Oberon, "this is the same Athenian."

"This is the woman," replied Puck, "but not this the man!"

Oberon realized that Puck had made a mistake: Demetrius still loved Hermia, who still loved Lysander – but now, Lysander loved Helena, who still loved Demetrius!

Demetrius was overcome with exhaustion and lay down to rest, while Hermia plunged into the nearest thicket in search of Lysander.

"What hast thou done?" cried Oberon, annoyed by his sprite's mistake. He sent Puck to fetch Helena.

"I go, I go; look how I go," cried Puck.

Meanwhile Oberon anointed Demetrius's weary eyelids with the flower's juice. "When his love he doth espy, let her shine as gloriously as the Venus of the sky," he whispered.

At that moment, Puck returned, drawing Helena along behind him with an invisible thread. Lysander followed her, still bewitched and lovesick!

Demetrius awoke, and when his eyes rested on Helena it was as if he was seeing her for the first time. The arrow of love pierced his heart and he threw himself at her feet. "O Helena, goddess, nymph, perfect, divine!"

Helena, far from being happy, believed Demetrius was mocking her. "O spite! O hell!" she cried. "I see you all are bent to set against me for your merriment."

When Hermia arrived on this scene, she quickly understood that both Lysander and Demetrius now loved Helena. Hermia was beside herself with anger, and screamed abuse at her friend. "O me! You juggler! You canker-blossom! You thief of love!"

"You puppet, you!" retaliated Helena.

"Thou painted maypole!" shrieked Hermia, flying at Helena, her nails like a cat's claws.

Lysander and Demetrius looked on, and when they could bear it no more they went to find space for their own duel.

Left to themselves, Hermia and Helena couldn't wait to get away from each other.

"I will not trust you, nor longer stay in your curst company," declared Helena, using her long legs to vanish into the wood.

"This is thy negligence," Oberon declared to Puck as he came out of the shadows.

"Believe me, King of Shadows, I mistook," protested Puck – although he was enjoying every minute of the drama! However, Oberon wanted the harm that the magic had done to be undone with another magic flower. So on Oberon's orders, Puck drew the lovers into the wood.

"Up and down, up and down," he sang, "I will lead them up and down." Puck led the lovers this way and that way, through bush and briar. They could hear each other, but they could not see each other. At last, thoroughly confused and exhausted, they fell asleep – all within the same glade. Puck was delighted with his work!

As Puck squeezed the flower's juice on Lysander's eyes, he sang:

"When thou wak'st,

Thou taks't

True delight

In the sight

Of thy former lady's eye!

Jack shall have Jill; nought shall go ill."

With these words, Puck left the sleeping lovers and vanished to watch what would happen when they awoke.

For once, Puck had not caused more mischief. Hermia woke to Lysander's love and Helena to Demetrius's. All anger was forgotten as these young Athenians were reunited in both friendship and love.

Meanwhile, in another part of the wood, Bottom lay sleeping in Titania's loving arms. Oberon looked down at them with amusement and then put an antidote on Titania's eyelids. "See as thou was wont to see," he whispered.

Then he woke Titania. She was mortified that Oberon had found her with a snoring ass in her arms! "My Oberon, what visions have I seen! Methought I was enamour'd of an ass," she cried. To cover her confusion she promised to give the changeling boy to Oberon. Oberon was satisfied at last! He called for music and danced happily away with Titania, leaving Puck to turn Bottom back to his usual self.

The day was nearly dawning and Duke Theseus was leading his hounds on an early morning hunt with his love, Hippolyta, and Hermia's father, Egeus. When they came across the runaway lovers, Egeus was still eager to force Hermia to marry Demetrius! "I beg the law!" he demanded of Duke Theseus.

Luckily for Hermia, this was Duke Theseus's wedding day. When he saw the young people so in love and paired off so happily, he overruled Egeus. He bade the whole party return with him to Athens and resolved that all three couples would wed that very day: he and Hippolyta, Hermia and Lysander, and Helena and Demetrius. Everyone was delighted, except Egeus, who grumbled all the way home!

After the wedding ceremonies, the motley troupe of actors – including Bottom,

who had his old head back – were called to put on their play. They put their all into every part! "Roar!" went the lion and "shine" went the moon, so that the audience cried, "Well roared, Lion" and "Well shone, Moon." The play earned them much money and applause!

As the players departed, the duke called for music and everyone celebrated the end of an eventful day with a dance. Even Egeus smiled – he seemed quite pleased that his daughter was neither dead nor banished but dancing in the arms of Lysander, the man she truly loved.

"The iron tongue of midnight hath told twelve," yawned the duke, as the music faded. "Lovers to bed; 'tis almost fairy time."

And so the whole company, at last restored to happy harmony, retired to bed.

For a moment the hall was left in quiet darkness. Then came the fairy king and queen, attended by Puck and a whole train of fairies, elves and goblins, and they banished the darkness with fairy light. They had come to bless the palace of Duke Theseus and all who slept there – a perfect end to the story, or maybe to a midsummer night's dream in an enchanted wood…

If we shadows have offended,
Think but this and all is mended.
That you have but slumber'd here,
While these visions did appear.
So, good night unto you all.

Macbeth

On a foul, bleak night, rain lashed across the Scottish heath, and through the roaring thunder and cracking lightning came an unearthly cry: "When shall we three meet again? In thunder, lightning, or in rain?"

"When the hurlyburly's done," came the answer. "When the battle's lost and won."

"Where the place?"

"Upon the heath."

"There to meet with Macbeth," said a third voice.

The following morning, the beating of a drum echoed across the same bleak landscape. Closer and closer it came to the place where the unearthly cries had been heard. The drum beat heralded Macbeth and Banquo, two Scottish generals returning home to Inverness. They had just defeated an army of rebels who had risen against Macbeth's cousin, King Duncan. Few had ever seen such courage as the two generals had shown in the battle. It was said that Macbeth had brandished his sword with such speed that it smoked with the blood of his enemies. Certainly, both men were so stained with blood that even the pouring rain could not remove it.

"So foul and fair a day I have not seen," shouted Macbeth against the storm.

Suddenly, as if from nowhere, three weird creatures rose out of the gloom. Both men stopped in their tracks.

"What are these, so wither'd and so wild in their attire?" gasped Banquo.  The creatures seemed to be women, but they had beards. Were they real or were the generals imagining them?

"Are you aught that man may question?" asked Banquo. He had heard that there were witches living on the heath who could tell you your future.

The three witches, if that is what they were, put their bony fingers to their skinny lips as if to silence Banquo. They turned to Macbeth.

"All hail, Macbeth," cried the first. "Hail to thee, Thane of Glamis!"

Macbeth was taken aback – the first witch had addressed him correctly, but how did she know who he was?

"All hail, Macbeth! Hail to thee, Thane of Cawdor!" said the second, which was strange, as he was not the Thane of Cawdor.

Strangest of all was the third witch's greeting: "All hail, Macbeth, that shall be king hereafter!"

Maybe these were more than greetings – maybe these were prophesies. Banquo was excited at the possibility, and asked the witches to look into the seeds of time and say what his future held.

"Thou shalt get kings, though thou be none. So, all hail, Macbeth and Banquo!" said the witches. With that, they disappeared like bubbles into the chill air.

"Whither are they vanished?" asked Banquo, amazed.

Macbeth gave no answer, for already his mind was consumed with the idea that he might one day be King of Scotland!

Moments later, two messengers sent from King Duncan approached across the heath. They brought the news that the king had made Macbeth Thane of Cawdor in honour of his great victory. The two generals stood stunned – the witches' first prediction had come true already!

Macbeth turned to Banquo. "Do you not hope your children shall be kings, when those that gave the Thane of Cawdor to me promised no less to them?" he asked.

Banquo smiled at his friend. He was more cautious than Macbeth and less swayed by ambition, and he warned Macbeth that such creatures of the dark might have evil intent. They could be trying to trick Macbeth into some deed that would have dire consequences. But Macbeth brushed away the warning.

In the days that followed, Macbeth could think of nothing but the crown – the crown of Scotland that would sit on his head when he was the king! How soon would that be? he wondered. Should he be doing something to make sure it happened? No, he thought to himself. "If chance will have me king, why, chance may crown me, without my stir." But the seed of ambition had been sown by the three witches, and ambition is an evil master. Dark thoughts began to stir in Macbeth's mind – thoughts of ways he could hasten the day of his coronation.

When Banquo and Macbeth finally arrived at the palace, King Duncan could not have greeted them more warmly or with more gratitude for their great bravery.

"O worthiest Cousin! Welcome hither!" he cried. "I have begun to plant thee, and will labour to make thee full of growing. Noble Banquo, that hast no less deserved, let me infold thee and hold thee to my heart."

Such a greeting from the king would have swelled the hearts of most men, but not Macbeth's. For shortly afterwards, King Duncan named his son, Malcolm, heir to the throne of Scotland. This was the honour that Macbeth had been hoping to receive.

"Stars, hide your fires!" Macbeth muttered to himself. "Let not light see my black and deep desires."

King Duncan went on to say that he would visit Macbeth's castle at Inverness. Again, Macbeth should have been pleased by this honour. But he was consumed by the desire to be king and all he could think about was that Malcolm now stood in his way. Maybe he could not rely on chance to make him king ... maybe he would have to give chance a helping hand!

Macbeth couldn't wait to tell his wife all that had happened, so he sent a letter ahead to her. Her excitement grew as she read it, for she was even greedier for power than Macbeth. She could already see the golden crown of Scotland on her husband's head. Macbeth was ambitious, but he had a sense of honour. Lady Macbeth was quite ruthless and only honoured power and ambition. She was capable of destroying anyone who stood in her husband's way.

By the time Macbeth reached his castle, Lady Macbeth was already plotting King Duncan's death! When she greeted Macbeth she saw that his thoughts had also turned to murder, but she was worried by his lack of cunning. "Your face, my Thane, is as a book where men may read strange matters," she warned him. "Look like the innocent flower, but be the serpent under't."

Their talk was interrupted by the arrival of King Duncan and his two sons, Prince Malcolm and Prince Donalbain. The king was delighted by the sweet air around the castle, and by Lady Macbeth, who appeared so charming and welcoming.

But Lady Macbeth was secretly urging her husband to kill him that night.

In preparation for the evil deed, Lady Macbeth drugged King Duncan's two guards, who lay beside the king as he slept.

Now that murder had become a reality, Macbeth was agonizing over it. King Duncan was a good and gentle man, and a guest in Macbeth's house. It was his duty to protect the king, not to murder him.

"We will proceed no further in this business," he told his wife. "If we should fail?"

"Screw your courage to the sticking-place and we'll not fail!" Lady Macbeth scorned.

So, swayed by his wife, Macbeth reluctantly agreed to murder the king as he lay in bed that night. Lady Macbeth's evil heart swelled with satisfaction and she retired to her chamber to await the time.

Macbeth remained hunched in his chair, imagining the fearful deed that lay before him. His dark thoughts were interrupted by the arrival of Banquo and his son Fleance. Banquo had brought a gift from the king: a beautiful diamond for Lady Macbeth, whom King Duncan had called his "most kind hostess"! Macbeth inwardly groaned. Could he really murder this man, this king, this giver of gifts and sweet compliments?

"I dreamt last night of the three weird sisters," said Banquo. "To you they have show'd some truth."

"I think not of them," lied Macbeth, trying to end the conversation.

When Banquo left him, he dismissed the last of the servants and tried to prepare himself for the foul murder. He paced up and down the great hall, trying to gather courage, but then he saw a phantom dagger hovering in front of him. "Is this a dagger which I see before me, the handle toward my hand?" he cried.

Meanwhile, Lady Macbeth, fearing her husband's courage would fail him, had decided she would have to murder King Duncan herself.

She crept into his room and looked upon the sleeping guards. "That which hath made them drunk hath made me bold!" she whispered.

Satisfied that they would not wake, she took their daggers and raised them above the king. But just as she was about to plunge the daggers downwards she looked at his face and froze. King Duncan looked so like her own father that she felt her courage leave her. She dropped the daggers and fled from the room, shaken by her failure.

Lady Macbeth ran to find her husband, for time was running out and the guards would soon wake from their stupor. She waited outside while Macbeth crept into King Duncan's room.

Reluctantly, Macbeth picked up the daggers. Closing his eyes, he plunged them into King Duncan's heart. Then he ran from the room, his hands dark with the king's blood and the daggers still clenched in his fists.

"I have done the deed," he cried, overwhelmed with the horror of it.

"Why did you bring these daggers from the place?" cried Lady Macbeth. "They must lie there: go carry them, and smear the sleepy grooms with blood."

Macbeth would not go back – he was too afraid to see what he had done.

"Infirm of purpose!" cried Lady Macbeth, furiously. "Give me the daggers!"

She grabbed the daggers and ran to return them to the grooms, covering their hands and faces with blood for good measure.

Later, when King Duncan's body was found, the whole castle rocked with cries of "murder and treason!" For he was the most noble of sovereigns and was loved by all.

Macbeth's guilt made him feel that all eyes were upon him. He was terrified of being discovered so, claiming vengeance, he killed both the guards before they could be questioned and reveal their innocence. "O! Yet I do repent me of my fury, that I did kill them," he said.

Despite his display of grief, many suspected that Macbeth, aided by his wife, had murdered the king. The king's two sons feared for their own lives and decided to flee from Scotland, Malcolm to England and Donalbain to Ireland. So Macbeth, as next in line to the throne, was crowned King of Scotland. He had achieved his ambition and had also fulfilled the witches' third prophecy.

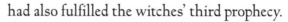

"Thou hast it now: king, Cawdor, Glamis, all, as the weird women promised," Banquo said to himself, "and I fear thou play'dst most foully for't."

Macbeth was haunted by the fear of being discovered as well as his own guilt. He worried that Banquo would find proof of the murder, or that somehow Banquo's descendants and not his own would one day reign, just as the witches had foretold.

"To be thus is nothing, but to be safely thus," he muttered to himself. "Our fears in Banquo stick deep."

Macbeth decided that the only way he could hold on to his crown and pass it on to his own children was to murder Banquo and his son, Fleance. To this end he invited all the local thanes to a feast. As Banquo and Fleance made their way to the palace, they were brutally attacked by Macbeth's hired assassins. Fleance managed to escape, but Banquo died.

"O, treachery! Fly, good Fleance, fly, fly, fly!" cried Banquo as he lay dying. "Thou mayst revenge."

Oblivious to this horrific deed, the other thanes were merrily dining with King Macbeth and his queen. Macbeth was tense and nervous, but tried to put aside his guilt. Then, just as he stood to give a toast, Banquo's bloody, wounded ghost appeared and silently sat down in Macbeth's seat.

"Which of you have done this?" asked Macbeth in horror.

But neither the thanes nor the queen could understand what he meant, as they could not see Banquo.

"Thou canst not say I did it," shouted Macbeth at the spectre. "Never shake thy gory locks at me."

There was an uncomfortable shuffling amongst the thanes and some made to leave.

"Why do you make such faces?" whispered his wife. "When all's done you look but on a stool."

Macbeth was so unnerved by the ghost and the wounds it bore, which had been inflicted by his own henchmen, that the queen finally dismissed their guests, pretending that the king was sometimes afflicted by strange visions.

From then on, both Macbeth and his queen suffered long, sleepless nights, filled with hideous dreams. Macbeth's wife, who had been so bold and ruthless, began to feel that she would never wash the blood of guilt from her hands. Yet both were still obsessed with keeping the throne. Macbeth decided to return to the heath to seek out the witches and ask them what the future held.

Macbeth set out across the heath on another night of thundering skies. He finally found the three witches in a cave, chanting over a cauldron of boiling hell-broth.

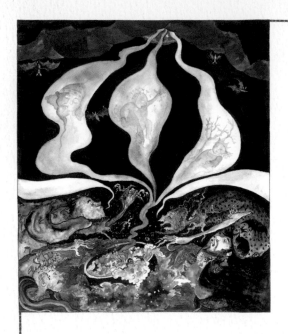

"Round about the cauldron go; in the poison'd entrails throw. Double, double toil and trouble; fire burn and cauldron bubble," they cried.

As Macbeth stood watching, three apparitions rose from the cauldron: the first was an armed head which warned Macbeth to beware of Macduff, the Thane of Fife; the second was a bloody child who told Macbeth that no man born of woman could harm him; the third was another child, wearing a crown and holding a tree, who reassured Macbeth that he would not be vanquished until Great Birnam Wood came to Dunsinane Hill, where Macbeth's castle stood.

When Macbeth asked if Banquo's heirs would reign, the cauldron sank into the ground and eight ghostly kings passed by, followed by Banquo's ghost. The last king carried a mirror which showed many more kings, and Macbeth knew that they were Banquo's descendants. It was as he had feared – Banquo's son Fleance had escaped.

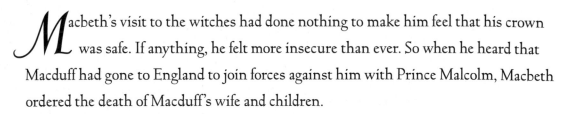

Macbeth's visit to the witches had done nothing to make him feel that his crown was safe. If anything, he felt more insecure than ever. So when he heard that Macduff had gone to England to join forces against him with Prince Malcolm, Macbeth ordered the death of Macduff's wife and children.

A messenger carried this terrible news to Macduff in England. He was stunned. He heard the words but could hardly believe the horror of such a deed.

"All my pretty ones? Did you say all?" he cried. "What, all my pretty chickens and their dam at one fell swoop?" Nothing would ever wipe out the desolation of such a loss, but Macduff swore to have his revenge.

"Let's make us medicines of our great revenge, to cure this deadly grief," said Malcolm. They were determined to reclaim the crown from such an unworthy king.

This terrible murder of innocent children and their mother lost Macbeth many friends. He and his wife began to feel increasingly isolated, and their guilt grew. Though Queen Macbeth, as she now was, had the crown she had longed for, her life had become a living nightmare. She wandered the castle trying to wash away the blood of King Duncan from her hands and clothes – blood that had long gone, but blood that haunted her still. "Out, damned spot! Out I say!" she would cry.

After days and nights of the queen not sleeping or eating, her servant called the court doctor. But he had no medicines to ease a guilty mind.

"Here's the smell of the blood still," cried the queen, as the doctor and waiting woman looked on helplessly. "All the perfumes of Arabia will not sweeten this little hand. Oh, oh, oh!"

Eventually, Lady Macbeth was unable to bear the ghastly visions any more, and she died. Macbeth now felt more hated and alone than ever. His wife had been his guiding force, his partner in crime. "She should have died hereafter," he groaned. "There would have been time for such a word."

*M*acbeth was still reeling from his wife's death when a soldier who had been on watch approached him.

"I should report that which I say I saw, but know not how to do it," he said nervously.

"Well, say, sir," cried Macbeth impatiently. "I looked towards Birnam, and anon, methought, the wood began to move."

"Liar, and slave!" cried Macbeth, furiously.

But the watch was not a liar, for thousands of Prince Malcolm's troops were fast approaching, shielded behind branches cut from Great Birnam Wood. Thus it appeared that the wood moved towards Dunsinane Hill and Macbeth's castle – the event the witches said would precede Macbeth's downfall.

Macbeth still believed himself invulnerable – even if Great Birnam Wood appeared to be moving towards his castle, he knew he would never be killed in battle. Hadn't the witches said that no man of woman born would ever kill him? So, gathering his courage, he rallied his remaining forces and waged a bloody war against Malcolm's army, until Macduff spotted him.

"Turn, hell-hound, turn!" cried Macduff, his sword held high.

Macbeth turned and as their swords clashed, Macbeth cried out, "Let fall thy blade on vulnerable crests; I bear a charmed life, which must not yield to one of woman born."

"Despair thy charm," cried Macduff in triumph. "Macduff was from his mother's womb untimely ripped!"

Macbeth's sword slackened in his hand. Macduff had not been born by natural means – he had been taken from his mother's womb by surgeons. Macbeth knew that this meant his end had come. Macduff, with all the pain of his lost family in his sword, made sure his enemy's death was swift and bloody. With one sword stroke, he parted Macbeth's head from his body and then carried it to Prince Malcolm, the rightful heir to King Duncan's throne.

"Hail, King! For so thou art!" cried Macduff, triumphantly, "Hail, King of Scotland!"

So Prince Malcolm claimed back his father's throne and the Scottish people rejoiced. The wicked reign of Macbeth and his ambitious wife had ended, just as had been prophesied. Scotland was at peace, ruled once more by a true and noble king.

Hail, King of Scotland!

As You Like It

Many years ago, there was a province in France ruled over by wicked Duke Frederick. His court was not a happy place, for he was greedy, jealous and quick of temper. He had stolen his brother's dukedom and banished him from court without a franc to his name. His brother, Duke Senior, had made his home in the Forest of Arden, and many loyal courtiers had followed him there. They all enjoyed the forest life and lived like Robin Hood and his merry men, making their homes amongst the trees and feasting on deer and forest fruits. They didn't miss court life one jot, even in the wintertime.

The only person that Duke Senior missed was his daughter, Rosalind, who had not been exiled with him. Rosalind had been allowed to stay at court to keep Duke Frederick's only child, Celia, company. At first Rosalind had been happy, but now that she and Celia had become young women, Duke Frederick had taken against her and was often unkind. He felt that she outshone his own daughter in beauty and wit, and longed for an excuse to send her from court. Poor Rosalind began to miss her father terribly and there were days when she could hardly raise a smile. This day was one of them, and neither her dear cousin nor Touchstone the jester could comfort her.

"I pray thee, Rosalind, sweet my coz, be merry," begged Celia.

"Dear Celia, I show more mirth than I am mistress of," sighed Rosalind.

"Stand you both forth now," tried Touchstone as he turned a somersault. "Stroke your chins, and swear by your beards that I am a knave."

It was no good – neither friend managed to raise a smile from Rosalind.

Then a courtier named Le Beau arrived with the news that Monsieur Charles, a fearsome giant wrestler, was taking on all comers in the palace courtyard. He had already broken the ribs of three opponents and was about to take on a fourth – a young, handsome fellow, according to Le Beau. With yet another sad sigh, Rosalind agreed to watch the event with her cousin. Neither of them were really keen on wrestling, but they thought it might be a distraction … until they saw the young man who was about to fight Charles. Then they were horrified! Certainly he was good looking, but he was also light of build and no match for Charles. Rosalind and Celia begged him not to enter the ring, for he would surely be crushed to death.

"Give over this attempt," said Celia.

"Do, young sir," pleaded Rosalind, who felt faint at the thought of this handsome youth being hurt – she was already quite taken with him.

However, Orlando – for that was his name – needed the prize money, and would not be dissuaded. Besides, he found Rosalind as attractive as she found him and was determined to show off his strength to her.

"The little strength that I have, I would it were with you," declared Rosalind.

Celia and Rosalind had been right – Orlando was no match for Charles in strength and size. When he first entered the ring, it seemed certain he would be flung through the ropes with broken limbs. Yet Orlando was much quicker on his feet than the lumbering giant and he was soon running circles around him, ducking and diving beneath Charles's powerful arms. Orlando suddenly moved behind the giant and then skilfully floored him. Everyone cheered.

"O excellent young man!" cried Rosalind, jumping up and down with excitement.

Even grumpy Duke Frederick was full of praise for Orlando – until he learned that Orlando's father had been his old enemy, Sir Rowland de Boys.

"I would thou hadst told me of another father," he growled in disgust.

The duke threw the winner's purse at Orlando's feet and marched off in a fury. The whole court fled nervously after him, except for Rosalind, who was unwilling to part from Orlando. Fearing that he might vanish out of her life for ever, she gave him a parting gift – the gold chain from around her neck. "Gentleman," she smiled, "wear this for me."

Orlando would have answered, but he was tongue-tied with love. Before he could find the right words, Le Beau returned to urge him to leave court immediately. The duke was in a dangerous mood and was threatening to have him killed. So Orlando fled, clutching Rosalind's gold chain and wondering if he would ever see her again.

Unfortunately, Orlando was not the only target of Duke Frederick's wrath. He had seen Rosalind talking to Orlando and assumed they were plotting against him. So a little later, while Celia and Rosalind were discussing the handsome Orlando, Duke Frederick marched in on them like an angry bear.

"Mistress," he growled, pointing at Rosalind, "dispatch you with your safest haste, and get you from our court."

"Me, Uncle?" asked poor Rosalind.

"You, Cousin," said the duke. "Within these ten days if that thou be'st found so near our public court as twenty miles – thou diest for it."

Both Celia and Rosalind gasped at the duke's harsh words. When Rosalind asked why she was being sent from court, the duke said being her father's daughter was reason enough. Celia said she couldn't live without her cousin, but Duke Frederick just scoffed and warned Rosalind again to get out of the court … or die!

Celia was horrified by her father's cruelty and determined not to be parted from her cousin. "I'll go along with thee," she said, clasping her cousin's hand.

So the cousins resolved to go and find Rosalind's father in the Forest of Arden. As it would not be safe for two girls to travel through the forest alone, they decided to disguise themselves: Rosalind as a poor youth, Ganymede, and Celia as his sister, a

country maid named Aliena. "And therefore look you call me Ganymede," laughed Rosalind, quite excited by the idea of cutting her hair and donning boy's clothing.

"No longer Celia, but Aliena," smiled her cousin, also delighted by the plan.

They agreed to take Touchstone with them for extra protection, and they hurried off to prepare for their adventure.

Meanwhile, Orlando returned to the home he shared with his older brother, Oliver – but he was greeted at the door by his loyal, elderly servant, Adam, who was greatly agitated.

"Why, what's the matter?" asked Orlando.

"O unhappy youth," cried the old man. "Come not within these doors! Your brother means to burn the lodging where you lie. Abhor it. Fear it. Do not enter it."

"What, would'st thou have me go and beg my food?" cried Orlando, for he had no money except what he had won that day. Oliver, who had always been jealous of Orlando, had stolen Oliver's share of their dead father's estate.

"I have five hundred crowns," said the old man. "Let me go with you."

So Ganymede, Aliena and Touchstone were not the only ones to flee to the Forest of Arden that day. Hot on their heels were Orlando and Adam, one as lithe as a young sapling and the other as old and gnarled as an ancient oak. All of them were hoping to find refuge with Duke Senior – if only they could find him!

When Duke Frederick discovered that Celia had run away with Rosalind, he was distraught. He sent messengers to search for Celia, but as none of them knew that they were searching for a maiden named Aliena accompanied by a youth named Ganymede,

they failed to find her. So when the duke heard that Orlando and Adam had also fled to Arden, he sent for Oliver and ordered him to search for his brother. He hoped that Orlando might lead Oliver to Celia and Rosalind. Oliver set out to search the forest, for to disobey Duke Frederick meant certain death.

In the meantime, Rosalind, Celia and Touchstone had reached the forest. It seemed very big and dark, with paths leading in every direction. They all felt rather afraid.

"O Jupiter!" moaned Rosalind. "How weary are my spirits."

"I care not for my spirits if my legs were not weary," said Touchstone.

"I pray you, bear with me," puffed Celia. "I cannot go no further."

The three travellers fell to the ground in an exhausted heap, wondering where they might spend the night and how they would feed themselves. Luckily for them, a passing shepherd offered them some food and a cottage to rent. They were overwhelmed with relief and decided to rest before beginning their search for Rosalind's father.

Celia looked around the little house. "I like this place, and willingly could waste my time in it," she declared. With that, she threw herself down on one of the little beds and promptly fell asleep.

Orlando and Adam also felt tired and hungry by the time they reached the forest.

"I die for food," cried the aged Adam.

Orlando sniffed the air – was that venison he could smell cooking? He decided to follow his nose. As fortune would have it, the smell did indeed lead to a joint of venison roasting over a fire in Duke Senior's camp. The duke made both men welcome.

As Orlando feasted and Adam slowly recovered, one of the duke's courtiers

All the world's a stage, and all the men and women merely players: they have their exits and their entrances; and one man in his time plays many parts, his acts being seven ages.

entertained them with a speech. The speech went on and on and finally sent Adam to sleep, but Orlando joined in the applause and general merriment that followed.

As Orlando chatted to the duke, he explained that he was the son of Sir Rowland de Boys. Duke Senior was delighted, for unlike his brother Frederick, he had been a firm friend of Orlando's father. "Be truly welcome hither," he cried. "I am the duke that loved your father."

So Orlando and Adam made their home in Duke Senior's forest camp. They were happy there, but Orlando was still pining for his love, Rosalind.

Every day on the other side of the forest, Rosalind, still dressed as Ganymede, wandered through the trees searching in vain for her father. But although she longed to find him, she longed to see Orlando again even more. She was so preoccupied with thinking about Orlando that she hardly noticed that scraps of paper had mysteriously begun to appear on the branches of the trees. Then one day, thinking she was plucking a leaf, she pulled one from a bush. She was astonished to see that it was a love poem!

"From the east to western Ind," she read, "No jewel is like Rosalind…" She gasped in delight – whoever wrote this poem must love her!

As she rushed to show Celia what she had found, she was brought to a sudden stop, for there, in a clearing, was the author of the poem – Orlando! He was lying with pen and paper struggling over another verse. Celia was watching him from behind a tree.

"It is young Orlando, that tripped up the wrestler's heels and your heart both, in an instant," she whispered, pulling Rosalind into the shelter of the tree.

"Orlando?" gasped Rosalind, looking down at her boy's clothes. "Alas the day! What shall I do with my doublet and hose?"

Then she had an idea: she would introduce herself to Orlando as Ganymede and pretend to be a boy until she was sure Orlando loved her. So, putting on her most laddish air, she went up to Orlando and tried to engage him in conversation.

Orlando could hardly answer Ganymede's greeting, so lovesick was he for Rosalind. "I am he that is so love-shaked," he said, sighing. "I pray you, tell me your remedy."

"I could cure you, if you would but call me Rosalind, and come every day to my cottage and woo me," smiled Ganymede.

"Now, by the faith of my love, I will," promised Orlando, not realizing he was speaking to his Rosalind at that very moment!

Rosalind and Celia were delighted with this trick. As the days went by, they found they so enjoyed Orlando's company that they quite neglected their search for Rosalind's father. Every day, Orlando came to their cottage and wooed Rosalind – who was pretending to be Ganymede pretending to be Rosalind!

"Am not I your Rosalind?" Ganymede would say.

"I take some joy to say you are, because I would be talking of her," Orlando replied.

"Well, in her person I say I will not have you."

"Then in my own person I die."

Celia would sigh at these exchanges, for she longed to love and be loved like her cousin. Even Touchstone had found love in the forest – he was smitten with a goatherd of doubtful looks named Audrey.

Then one day, as Orlando was making his way to visit Ganymede, he came across a man asleep under a tree. He was shaken out of his dreams of Rosalind at once, for he saw that a venomous snake was coiled about the man's neck. Luckily the snake slipped away when it saw Orlando approach, but in the nearby bushes lurked a deadlier

danger – a hungry lion was preparing to pounce. Orlando looked at the man more closely and suddenly realized that it was Oliver! Did he really want to rescue his cruel brother from this fate? For the sake of his dear, dead father he decided he

must. Orlando hurled himself at the leaping lion and threw it to the ground, just as he had done with the wrestler, Charles. The lion had far larger claws and teeth than the wrestler, but Orlando bravely struggled with it until at last the lion lay dead.

When Oliver awoke and discovered what had happened, he felt ashamed at the way he had treated Orlando. He apologized and promised to change his ways, so with tears and hugs, the brothers were reunited. Orlando still wanted to visit Ganymede's cottage, but the lion had torn flesh from his arm and he had lost a good deal of blood. So Oliver helped his brother back to Duke Senior's camp where Orlando's wound was bandaged and Oliver was given fresh clothes. Orlando was still too weak to set off to meet Ganymede, so while he recovered he sent Oliver ahead to explain the delay.

"He sends this bloody napkin," said Oliver, when he arrived at the cottage. Rosalind took one look at her sweetheart's blood and fell to the ground in a faint.

"Many will swoon when they do look on blood," said Oliver, although he thought it rather odd behaviour for a young man.

Celia, dressed as Aliena, gave Oliver a little smile, for Rosalind was not the only one to feel faint – her legs were growing weaker by the moment as she looked at Orlando's handsome brother. As for Oliver, he thought Aliena the most beautiful young maiden he had ever set eyes upon. In fact, as the pair gazed into each other's eyes, they realized they were head over heels in love!

Oliver raced back to tell Orlando all about Aliena, his heart pounding every inch of the way. "I love Aliena; she loves me," he blurted out.

Oliver asked Orlando for his blessing. He said he would give Orlando their father's fortune and estate, and that he would live in the woods with Aliena and become a shepherd.

Orlando, no stranger to instant love himself, was delighted. "You have my consent. Let your wedding be tomorrow," he cried.

Suddenly, Orlando's heart felt very heavy – for now that Oliver had found love, Orlando pined for Rosalind even more. Where was she? Would he ever see her again? All he had to hold on to was her gold chain.

"O, how bitter a thing it is to look into happiness through another man's eyes," he cried, as he watched his brother rush off into the arms of Aliena.

*T*he following morning, as Orlando had promised, the duke and all his party gathered in a leafy glade for Oliver's wedding. Two pages sang a welcome and guided the priest to the secret woodland chapel. Oliver was tingling with excitement as he waited for his bride to arrive, but the wedding was interrupted when Ganymede suddenly appeared. He approached Orlando and asked him if he would vow to marry Rosalind, should she be found.

"That would I," sighed Orlando.

Then Ganymede turned to Duke Senior. "You will bestow Rosalind on Orlando?" he asked.

"That would I," said the duke, wishing he could see his daughter again.

"I have promised to make all this matter even," Ganymede cried. "From hence I go!" With that, he vanished mysteriously into the undergrowth.

There was a shuffling of feet amongst the wedding guests. Everyone wondered what to expect next. They didn't have to wait long, for after a few minutes they heard music drifting towards them, and Touchstone and Audrey appeared, skipping through the trees. Then came Hymen, the god of marriage, who, to everyone's delight, was leading Rosalind and Celia, dressed once more as themselves. Duke Senior was overjoyed to see his daughter, and Orlando and Oliver embraced their transformed loves.

In the midst of all this happiness, a messenger came from Duke Frederick to say that he had repented of his wicked ways and wished to return the crown to his brother, the rightful duke. So it was time for everyone to return home. But first Hymen blessed the happy couples, and everyone sang and danced for one last day and night in the mysterious Forest of Arden.

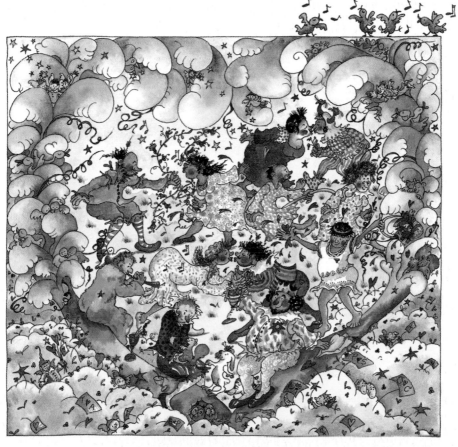

Romeo and Juliet

In the beautiful old Italian city of Verona, Lord Capulet was planning a grand banquet. All the noble families in the city were invited – all except the Montague family. The Capulets and Montagues were sworn enemies. They had been feuding for as long as anyone could remember, and their quarrel ran so deep that even their servants fought. If a member of the Capulet household passed a member of the Montague household on the street, the peaceful city would suddenly erupt in violence. The Prince of Verona was no longer prepared to tolerate this situation. He had decreed that the next Capulet or Montague to disturb the peace would pay with his life.

Lord Capulet had invited all the fairest ladies of Verona to the banquet including his own niece, Rosaline. She had many suitors, but unknown to Lord Capulet, the most passionate of all was a young nobleman named Romeo, son of his enemy, Lord Montague! Romeo was a romantic young man. His infatuation with Rosaline caused him much heartache, for Rosaline was a faithful Montague and scorned Romeo.

Day and night, Romeo was either wandering the streets of Verona looking for Rosaline or boring his friends, Benvolio and Mercutio, with tales of her great beauty. So when they heard that she would be at Lord Capulet's party, they persuaded Romeo to go with them, disguised behind a mask. They hoped to show him that there were many ladies in Verona who were even fairer than Rosaline. "Compare her face with some that I shall show, and I will make thee think thy swan a crow," said Benvolio.

Old Lord Capulet was in a jovial mood on the evening of his party. "Welcome gentlemen! Ladies that have their toes unplagued with corns will walk about with you. Come musicians, play!" he said.

He encouraged all the young folk to enjoy the dancing, including his daughter, Juliet, who soon took to the floor with a dashing knight. She was so merry and so very pretty that even the love-struck Romeo noticed her. Indeed, not realizing that she was Lord Capulet's daughter, Romeo suddenly found that his heart no longer belonged to Rosaline, but to Juliet! "O, she doth teach the torches to burn bright! Did my heart love till now?" he breathed.

Romeo did not keep his feelings to himself, but, as if in a dream, stood declaring his new love to all about him. Unfortunately, Lord Capulet's fiery nephew, Tybalt, recognized his voice. "This, by his voice, should be a Montague," he angrily cried. "To strike him dead I hold it not a sin!"

Tybalt called for his sword and had it not been for Lord Capulet, who forbade fighting at his ball, the evening would certainly have ended in bloodshed. Lord Capulet insisted that Tybalt make Romeo welcome. Tybalt unwillingly sheathed his sword, but he swore he would take revenge on Romeo at some other time.

Romeo was quite unaware of this passing danger. He waited until Juliet stopped dancing and then began to woo her. Juliet was entranced by Romeo and even allowed him to steal a kiss, and their few minutes together seemed to them like hours.

When Juliet was called away by her mother, Romeo realized she was a Capulet, but he didn't care. And when Juliet's nurse told her that Romeo was a Montague, her heart was too full of love to take notice of a family feud. "My only love sprung from my only hate!" she cried.

As the party ended, Romeo and his friends set off to make merry elsewhere, but Benvolio and Mercutio soon found themselves walking along the road on their own.

Romeo, as if pulled by a thread, had turned back to Juliet's house. He climbed over the high orchard wall and stood hidden in the shadows, searching the house for signs of life. He knew he was risking death by being there, and his heart pounded. Then a light appeared at one of the windows and Juliet stepped onto the balcony.

"O, it is my love!" whispered Romeo. He hid behind a tree and listened as Juliet declared her love for him to the stars!

"O gentle Romeo. 'Tis but thy name that is my enemy. Thou art thyself though, not a Montague," she said.

To Romeo, Juliet looked more beautiful than the sun itself, and encouraged by her loving words, he revealed himself. Both knew the danger he was in, but they could not think of parting. They fell so deeply in love that they agreed to wed the following day – in secret, in case their feuding families tried to part them. In the heat of this new passion, Juliet quite forgot that she was betrothed to Paris, a noble of her father's choice.

Dawn was breaking when Juliet's nurse finally persuaded her back into her room. "Goodnight, goodnight! Parting is such sweet sorrow that I shall say goodnight till it be morrow!" cried Juliet as she ran inside.

Romeo raced straight to the monastery where his good friend Friar Laurence lived. The friar asked Romeo if he had some good news from Rosaline.

"Rosaline? I have forgot that name!" cried Romeo, joyously.

The friar was surprised to hear this, and even more surprised that Romeo had so quickly found a new love, for he had heard so much of Rosaline over the past weeks. However, Friar Laurence believed that Romeo's heart was true, so he agreed to marry Romeo to his Juliet. The friar was a friend to both the Montagues and the Capulets and hoped that the marriage would unite the families and end the years of feuding.

That very afternoon, Juliet joined Romeo at the chapel of the monastery and the happy sweethearts were wed.

Afterwards they parted as they knew they must until Friar Laurence had broken the news to their families. Both were impatient for the coming night when Romeo planned to climb the wall into the Capulet's orchard one last time, so that he could spend some stolen moments with his new bride.

When Romeo returned from his wedding at the chapel the streets of Verona were deserted, for it was the time of day when all people of sense rested in the cool of their homes. So Romeo was surprised to run into his friends Benvolio and Mercutio, who were arguing with Tybalt.

"Mercutio, thou consort'st with Romeo," cried Tybalt, spoiling for a fight.

The last thing on Romeo's mind was fighting; all his thoughts were consumed by love. Besides, he was now related to Tybalt by marriage and the name Capulet had suddenly become very dear to him. So Romeo did his best to calm Tybalt. But Tybalt was determined to take revenge on Romeo for gatecrashing Lord Capulet's party.

When Romeo refused to fight, Mercutio stepped in to fight in his place even though Romeo tried to stop him. "Tybalt, Mercutio, the prince expressly hath forbidden bandying in Verona streets!" Romeo cried.

His words had no effect. Tybalt and Mercutio clashed swords, and as Romeo stepped in to part them, Tybalt's sword plunged into Mercutio's chest.

"A plague o' both your houses! They have made worms' meat of me," cried Mercutio. The wound was fatal and soon poor Mercutio lay dead in Romeo's arms.

Mercutio's death sent Romeo into a sudden rage. He grabbed a rapier and lunged at Tybalt, and before Romeo even realized what he was doing, Tybalt also lay dead. As Romeo looked at Tybalt's lifeless body, his anger left him. But it was too late – he had killed his wife's cousin. "O! I am fortune's fool," he cried. Romeo knew that the Prince of Verona might condemn him to death if he was arrested, so he fled to the sanctuary of Friar Laurence's cell.

When the Prince of Verona heard that Romeo had been provoked, he did not condemn him to death. However, his patience with the feuding families was at an end, so he banished Romeo from Verona. Oh, unhappy Juliet! At first she was furious with Romeo and wept copious tears for her dead cousin. "O God! Did Romeo's hand shed Tybalt's blood? O serpent heart, hid with a flowering face!"

Then her thoughts turned to her new husband. "My husband lives, that Tybalt would have slain!" Her love for Romeo changed her tears of sorrow to tears of joy.

Romeo came to see Juliet that night. He quickly secured her forgiveness and held

her in his arms. Yet the night was tinged with sadness, not only because of the adventures of the day, but also because the lovers knew that they had to part and had no way of knowing when they would be together again.

The morning dawned far too soon for them. Juliet tried to persuade Romeo that the morning song of the larks was the nightly call of the nightingale. But the sky was streaked with morning light and they had to say farewell. As Romeo set out for Mantua, where he would be safe from arrest, he promised to take every opportunity to send Juliet his greetings. They both prayed that Friar Laurence would soon secure a pardon for Romeo and pacify their families.

When Romeo left Juliet, he promised that they would soon be reunited and all their troubles would be forgotten. Poor Romeo – if he had known of Lord Capulet's plan, he might not have been so sure. For before Friar Laurence had a chance to share the news of Romeo and Juliet's marriage, Lord Capulet told Juliet's suitor, Paris, that he could marry Juliet in a few days' time. He hoped that a wedding would cheer his daughter after her cousin's death.

In vain, Juliet pleaded with her father not to rush her into marriage. She pointed out that she was only thirteen years old, too young to get married! She reminded him that Tybalt had only just died, and said she was too distressed to find any joy in such a union. But Paris was a rich, noble suitor and her father was determined. No daughter in Verona could refuse her father, and Juliet did not dare reveal the true obstacle to the wedding: her marriage to Romeo.

With Romeo already on his way to Mantua, Juliet did not know what to do, so she ran to Friar Laurence to seek his advice. In desperation they agreed a devious and dangerous plot.

Juliet went home and, to her father's joy, agreed to marry Paris. The whole household began to bustle with preparations for this sudden wedding. Guests were invited, flowers arranged, furniture polished and gowns stitched. Then, just before Juliet was due to put on her wedding dress, she took a drug which would make her appear dead for forty-two hours.

When Juliet's nurse went to wake her, she thought at first that Juliet was in a deep sleep. "Why, lamb! Why, lady! Fie, you slug-a-bed!" she said. She tried to tease Juliet awake, then shake her awake, but the poor woman soon realized it was hopeless.

Juliet's family were devastated – they were convinced that Juliet was dead. The wedding party became a funeral procession. Juliet was carried to the family burial vault, from where, according to the friar's plan, Romeo would soon rescue her.

Unfortunately a messenger reached Romeo with the false news of Juliet's "death" before the friar's letter, which would have told him that she was only drugged. Poor Romeo, knowing nothing of the friar's plan, was thrown into the deepest despair. "Is it even so?" he cried in anguish. Only a moment earlier he had been full of joy and expectation, believing he would be reunited with Juliet, imagining their future happiness. Now he believed that both she and his dreams were dead.

Romeo called for a horse to be saddled while he went to a local apothecary to buy poison – he had decided to return to Verona and die beside his sweetheart. "Well, Juliet, I will lie with thee tonight!" he cried, as he set off to see her for the last time.

It was midnight when Romeo arrived at the graveyard where the Capulets' tomb lay. The mourners were long departed and only the yew trees stood sentinel beside the tomb. Then out of the darkness came the weeping figure of Paris. He had come to throw flowers on Juliet's grave on what would have been their wedding night. Paris recognized Romeo at once. He knew he was a Montague and thought that he must have come to cause mischief at his enemies' tomb.

Romeo was not looking for a fight and longed to be left alone to die at Juliet's side. When Paris tried to apprehend him, Romeo tried to shake him off, but Paris was like an angry jackal and would not set him free. And so they fought. Romeo stabbed Paris, who fell backwards upon the rough ground.

"O, I am slain! If thou be merciful, open the tomb, lay me with Juliet," Paris begged.

"In faith, I will," cried the unhappy Romeo.

Romeo opened the tomb and gazed upon Juliet with so much love and sorrow that he hardly needed poison to stop his breaking heart. He lifted Paris in his arms and lay him beside her. Then he gazed upon his true love's face.

"Death, that hath sucked the honey of thy breath, hath had no power yet upon thy beauty," he said. He gave her one last kiss. "Here's to my love!" he said, drinking the poison. "O true apothecary! Thy drugs are quick. Thus with a kiss I die."

At that moment, Friar Laurence arrived at the graveyard, spade, lantern and crowbar in hand. He had only recently discovered that his letter had not reached Romeo, and his first thought was to rush and save Juliet from her tomb. Then he planned to find Romeo and tell him the joyous news that his love was still alive. As his old feet stumbled through the graves, he thought he saw a lantern flicker by the Capulets' tomb. Could it be Romeo? Had he arrived too late? "O! much I fear some ill unlucky thing," he muttered.

He entered the tomb and saw both Paris and Romeo dead beside the sleeping Juliet. "Romeo! Alack, alack!" the friar cried out, disturbing Juliet's unnatural sleep.

"O, comfortable friar, where is my lord?" she asked, as she awoke.

"Thy husband in thy bosom there lies dead; and Paris too," said Friar Laurence.

Hearing the night watch approach, Friar Laurence urged Juliet to flee with him before they were blamed for the death of both young men. But Juliet would not leave Romeo. She kissed his lips, hoping to find some poison there, but there was none.

Quickly, before the watch could stop her, Juliet picked up Romeo's dagger and stabbed herself. "O happy dagger. This is thy sheath; there rest and let me die!" she cried. Then she fell upon her beloved Romeo's body and died.

When the Montagues and Capulets arrived upon this tragic scene, they were grief stricken. The friar was summoned by the Prince of Verona and he related the whole story; how Romeo and Juliet had fallen in love; how he had married the pair hoping that their union would end their families' bitter feud; how his letter to Romeo had been delayed. The Prince of Verona rebuked Lord Capulet and Lord Montague for their feud, as it was this and not the friar's plan which was the true cause of this tragedy. "Never was a story of more woe than this of Juliet and her Romeo," he said.

The two old enemies were overcome with sorrow and guilt.

"Poor sacrifices of our enmity," wept Lord Montague.

"O brother Montague!" cried Lord Capulet, "give me your hand."

The grieving fathers each vowed to raise a golden statue to the other's child. Thus they buried their feud along with their precious children, Romeo and his sweet Juliet.

The Tempest

Many years ago, off the shore of a small, mystical isle, a ship struggled in the eye of a terrible tempest. The thunder roared, the lightning cracked and the waves raised the ship up towards the stormy clouds. There it seemed to rest for a moment, only to be dashed down into the brink by the raging sea. No ship could survive such a battering. No sailor could survive in such waters.

From the island, Miranda, a young and very beautiful girl, watched in horror as the ship fought to survive and the sailors cried out in fear. Sitting beside Miranda was her loving father, Prospero, his cloak flapping in the wind and his great staff held out towards the storm. He had been preparing for this moment for years. From his cell-like dwelling on the island, Prospero had been developing his magic powers from a rare book. Now his skill was so great that he could even control the elements.

Miranda suspected that her father had caused the storm, but had no idea why such a gentle man should wish to harm anyone. "If by your art, my dearest father, you have put the wild waters in this roar, allay them," she pleaded, clutching at his arm.

"Be collected," replied her father. "No more amazement. Tell your piteous heart there's no harm done. 'Tis time I should inform thee farther. Lend thy hand and pluck my magic garment from me." Prospero laid his cloak and great staff beside him and took his daughter's hands in his. "Canst thou remember a time before we came unto this cell?" he asked. "I do not think thou canst, for then thou wast not out three years old."

Bit by bit, Prospero revealed how he and Miranda had been cast away on the island, twelve years before. In those days, Prospero had been Duke of Milan, but he was always in his library studying his books and he left most of his duties to his brother Antonio. Eventually Antonio decided that if he was to do all the work, he should have Prospero's title as well! Aided by Alonso, King of Naples, he set about seizing the dukedom and getting rid of his brother. Prospero was very popular with the people of

Milan, so Antonio and King Alonso did not dare kill him outright. Instead they set him and his little daughter, Miranda, adrift in a tiny boat. Luckily Prospero's friend Gonzalo had secreted some clothes and other provisions on board, as well as Prospero's most precious books. These sustained the duke and his daughter until, after many long nights and days, they drifted to their island.

"Dost thou attend me?" Prospero asked Miranda as their history unfolded.

"Your tale, sir, would cure deafness," she replied in wonder.

Before Miranda and Prospero arrived on the island, the only inhabitants were Caliban, a monster, and some sprites which Caliban's mother, a foul witch, had trapped in trees before she died. Caliban, a strange and unearthly creature, became Prospero's servant, as did Ariel, an airy little sprite who was invisible to all but Prospero. Ariel had been freed from a tree by Prospero's magic and in return had promised to serve him faithfully for twelve years.

Because Miranda had lived nearly all her life on the island, she could not really remember ever seeing another human apart from her father. Now, Prospero told her, she was about to see that not all humans were as grey and aged as him; for along with the sailors, the storm-tossed ship had brought his friend Gonzalo, his enemies Antonio and King Alonso, and the king's son Prince Ferdinand to the island.

As Prospero was telling Miranda this, Ariel approached. Prospero put his magic cloak back on and, with a wave of his staff, he sent Miranda to sleep.

"Approach, my Ariel; come!" he called.

"All hail, great master, grave sir, hail! I come to answer thy best pleasure," replied the sprite.

Ariel was triumphant, for he had managed to rescue all those aboard the ship. He had brought the vessel safely into a hidden inlet and spirited everyone ashore, isolating all but Antonio, Gonzalo and King Alonso. Thanks to Ariel and Prospero's ingenuity, Prince Ferdinand thought his father must have drowned. Indeed, each man thought he was the only survivor of the tempest.

"But are they, Ariel, safe?" pressed Prospero, who had no desire to cause lasting harm.

"Not a hair perish'd," Ariel reassured him with pride.

Prospero smiled. He was pleased with the sprite, but told him there was still more work to be done.

"Is there more toil?" grumbled Ariel.

"How now? Moody?" admonished Prospero, sharply. "Dost thou forget from what a torment I did free thee?"

"No," sulked the sprite.

"If thou more murmur'st, I will rend an oak and peg thee in his knotty entrails till thou has howl'd away twelve winters!" threatened Prospero.

This was enough to make Ariel hang upon Prospero's every word! Off he went as ordered, in the guise of a sea nymph, to bring the young Prince Ferdinand to Prospero's cave.

Prospero then called upon Caliban to go and gather wood.

"There's wood enough within," grumbled Caliban.

"Hag-seed, hence!" snapped Prospero. "Fetch us in fuel; and be quick."

"I must obey: his art is of such power," said Caliban, who secretly longed for every toad, beetle and bat to land on his master.

Moments later, Ferdinand was drawn towards Prospero's cave by Ariel's singing. Miranda woke to a sight so new to her that she could only stare in wonder and delight.

"It carries a brave form: but 'tis a spirit," she murmured.

"No, wench," smiled her father. "It eats and sleeps, and hath such senses as we have."

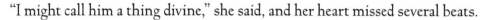

"I might call him a thing divine," she said, and her heart missed several beats.

Then Ferdinand saw Miranda and his heart also missed several beats! He had seen many fair faces, but never had he seen one to compare with Miranda's.

"O you wonder!" he gasped. "My prime request is if you be maid or no?"

"No wonder, sir," smiled Miranda, "but certainly a maid."

So it was that these two youngsters fell in love at this first meeting, just as Prospero had planned. Yet Prospero, thinking that love so easily and quickly come by might not last, decided to throw a few problems in their path. Adversity, he hoped, would seal their lovers' bond. With this aim, he accused Ferdinand of spying.

"Thou hast put thyself upon this island as a spy, to win it from me, the Lord on't," he charged Ferdinand.

"No, as I am a man," protested Ferdinand.

"There's nothing ill can dwell in such a temple," cried Miranda, devastated at her father's angry tone.

"Speak not you for him," snapped Prospero. "He's a traitor! Come, I'll manacle thy neck and feet together."

Prospero forbade Miranda to talk to Ferdinand, and set him to work shifting logs. Being a prince, Ferdinand

was not used to such labour, but he did it willingly to stay close to his new love.

Ferdinand hauled logs for hours, but as soon as Prospero's back was turned, Miranda went to offer him her help. "I'll bear your logs the while," she said.

"No, precious creature," puffed Ferdinand. "I had rather crack my sinews, break my back, than you should such dishonour undergo."

Ferdinand continued to move the logs and Miranda continued to distract him with her presence, so that each log took longer and longer to haul. The pair were so absorbed in each other that they failed to notice Prospero, who was hidden nearby, watching their love blossom. When he had seen enough to reassure himself of Ferdinand's good

intentions, he appeared suddenly, making them both jump. Miranda expected to be admonished for disobeying her father's orders and keeping company with Ferdinand, but Prospero smiled and turned to Ferdinand. "If I have too austerely punish'd you, your compensation makes amends – take my daughter," he said.

He then conjured up a flock of nymphs to sing a blessing on their engagement, and told them to rest and talk together all they liked, for he had work to do. Miranda and Ferdinand were delighted.

*M*eanwhile, down by the shore, Caliban was gathering driftwood, grumbling about Prospero all the while. "All the infections that the sun sucks up from bogs, fens, flats, on Prospero fall," he snarled.

Yet Caliban was terrified of Prospero's magic powers, and when a figure came along the beach, he was convinced that it was one of Prospero's sprites come to torment him. He hurriedly threw himself to the ground and hid under his cloak. "Lo now! Lo!" he cried in panic, "I'll fall flat."

However, the figure was no sprite – it was Trinculo, King Alonso's jester, who was wandering around the isle looking for other survivors of the shipwreck. He spied the cloak upon the ground with hideous limbs protruding from it at odd angles.

"What have we here?" he pondered. "A man or a fish? Dead or alive? A fish, he smells like a fish, a strange fish!"

Suddenly there was a crack of thunder. Trinculo feared another storm was coming and looked about for shelter. There was none – except Caliban's cloak. Trinculo forced himself to ignore the smell and the strange limbs and crawl under the stinking, ragged pile. "Misery acquaints a man with strange bedfellows," he cried.

Minutes later, Stefano, the king's drunken butler, fell over the heaving bundle. "This is some monster of the isle!" he cried in fright when Caliban poked his head out. Then Trinculo appeared and Stefano clapped his hands in delight. A friend from the ship at last, and one he could share a drink with!

Caliban, who was unaware of the shipwreck and who had never seen any humans apart from Prospero and Miranda, decided Trinculo and Stefano must be gods. "Hast thou not dropped from heaven?" he enquired.

"Out o' the moon, I do assure thee: I was the man in the moon, when time was," teased the drunken Stefano.

Caliban was as stupid as he was ugly and believed that, having come from the moon, they must be very powerful. He promised the pair that they would have the island for themselves and him as their slave, if only they would assassinate Prospero. "Thou shalt be lord of it," Caliban told Stefano eagerly.

It did not take much to persuade Stefano that being a king would be more fun than being a servant to a king, so he readily agreed. "Monster, I will kill this man," he declared, as though murder was no more trouble than taking another swig from his bottle of wine.

Ariel, who was hovering unseen above their drunken heads, overheard every word they said, and flew off to tell his master. So when the traitor Caliban and his companions drew near to Prospero's cave, Prospero was ready. Ariel had scattered Prospero's finest clothes in front of the cave, on the magician's orders. Then he and Prospero made themselves invisible and watched.

Caliban, Trinculo and Stefano crept rather noisily towards the cave, ready to kill Prospero. "Pray you, tread softly, that the blind mole may not hear a foot fall: we now are near his cell," whispered Caliban.

Just then, Caliban's foolish companions saw that they were treading on garments richly embroidered with gold and pearls – garments fit for a king. For a moment all thoughts of assassination left them.

"O King Stefano! Look what a wardrobe here is for thee!" cried out Trinculo.

"Put off that gown, Trinculo; by this hand, I'll have that gown," returned Stefano.

In no time at all, the drunken pair were dancing about, half-dressed in the courtly clothes, while Caliban pleaded with them to murder Prospero before they were all discovered and turned into barnacles. When Prospero saw that they were completely distracted, he unleashed his punishment: a pack of snarling phantom hounds. "Hey Mountain, hey! Fury, Fury! There, Tyrant, there! hark, hark!" shouted Prospero, waving his magic staff.

"Hark, they roar!" laughed Ariel.

"Let them be hunted soundly," ordered Prospero.

Ariel drove the dogs forward, and the terrified rascals ran before them. The trio were chased far off across the island until they collapsed into a pathetic heap, all breath and ambition worn out of them. Ariel dismissed the phantom hounds and returned to Prospero, another job well done.

*T*he time had come for the most important part of Prospero's plan: to settle the score with his brother and King Alonso. After the shipwreck, when King Alonso, Antonio and the good Gonzalo had unravelled themselves from the seaweed and wiped the sea salt from their eyes, they found, to their amazement, that they were quite unhurt. Their only distress was that the king's son, Ferdinand, who had been the first to throw himself out of the lurching ship, was not with them. They immediately set out in search of him. For hours they desperately combed the beaches, but they found no sign of Prince Ferdinand or any other survivors.

"He is drowned whom thus we stray to find," cried King Alonso, "and the sea mocks our frustrate search on land."

Gonzalo feared that the king was right and that the young prince had drowned, but he did not say so. "By your patience," he said instead, "I needs must rest me."

They were all tired, hungry and in despair, so the king consented to the old man's request. As the men dropped to the sand, they heard enchanting music. Strange beings materialized as if from nowhere, carrying a wonderful, richly scented feast.

This they lay in front of the weary men before vanishing as mysteriously as they had arrived. Prospero, cloaked in invisibility, stood by and watched.

"What were these?" wondered King Alonso – although hunger made him more eager to eat than think. "I will stand to and feed," he announced, deciding a throne might be more than he should expect.

Just as the three men were about to tuck into the delicious banquet, there was a rushing of wind and a clap of thunder and lightning. Ariel, disguised as a harpy, flapped his wings upon the table and the food vanished! "You fools!" he cried, and then, in shocking detail, he reminded them of their sins against Prospero and his innocent child.

Guilt and fear froze their spirits: everything the harpy accused them of was true. Their sins began to weigh heavily on them. Then Ariel, invisible once again, drew the unhappy nobles closer to Prospero's cell. There he led them into a magic circle, formed by Prospero, which held them like unwilling statues. Delighted, Prospero sent Ariel to fetch his old sword, hat and duke's robes.

When Ariel had helped Prospero into this attire, Prospero smiled. "Why, that's my dainty Ariel! I shall miss thee," he said. "But yet thou shall have freedom."

Then he appeared before his brother and King Alonso, dressed just as he would have been twelve years before. To their guilty minds, it appeared that Prospero had risen from the dead.

"Behold, Sir King, the wronged Duke of Milan, Prospero," he announced.

Even Gonzalo, who was innocent of all wrongdoing, gasped at this vision from their past. Could he be real, or would he vanish as strangely as he had appeared, like the phantom feast? When Prospero did not vanish and they realized that he was truly the

old duke, Antonio and King Alonso were awestruck into true repentance. They begged to be forgiven.

"Thy dukedom I resign, and do entreat thou pardon me my wrongs," said King Alonso.

Prospero ignored him for a moment as he went to embrace his noble friend Gonzalo, who had behaved with such honour. Then, since King Alonso and Antonio were truly repentant, Prospero's anger was finally placated.

"My dukedom since you have given me again, I will requite you with as good a thing," he said to King Alonso.

Prospero released the three men from the circle and led them to where Ferdinand and Miranda sat playing chess.

King Alonso hardly dared to believe his eyes. "If this prove a vision of the island, one dear son shall I twice lose," he said, shaking his head in disbelief.

Ferdinand jumped up and ran to kneel at his father's feet. "Though the seas threaten, they are merciful: I have curs'd them without cause," he cried in relief.

King Alonso touched his son's head and, finding he was not a vision of his imagination, raised him from the ground and embraced him warmly.

"What is this maid, with whom thou wast at play?" he enquired. "Is she the goddess that hath sever'd us?"

"Sir, she is mortal," smiled Ferdinand, "but by immortal Providence she's mine."

Ferdinand then told King Alonso that he wished to marry Miranda. "I chose her when I could not ask my father," he explained.

Seeing Miranda's beauty and his son's happiness, the king gave his consent. Like Prospero, he hoped the union would heal the rift between Milan and Naples. "Let grief and sorrow still embrace his heart that doth not wish you joy!" he cried.

"Be it so," said old Gonzalo, warmly. "Amen!"

Into the midst of their rejoicing, Caliban, Trinculo and Stefano arrived, urged on by Ariel. They were still a little the worse for drink, still in their stolen apparel, and still moving slowly and with great difficulty.

"I have been in such a pickle," moaned Trinculo.

"I am not Stefano, but a cramp," groaned Stefano.

"I shall be pinch'd to death," grumbled Caliban.

It would be true to say that no one felt sorry for the strange looking trio. Strangest of all was Caliban, for none of the nobles had ever seen his like before. Now that his dukedom had been restored, Prospero was of a mind to forgive these would-be assassins too, but only in return for a little hard labour.

"Go, sirrah, to my cell," he ordered Caliban. "Take with you your companions: as you look to have my pardon, trim it handsomely."

So they did, for even Caliban had grown a little wiser and would not risk upsetting Prospero again.

The rest of the party then made themselves comfortable, while Prospero entertained them with tales of his and Miranda's adventures over the past twelve years. The following morning they all planned to sail to Naples to celebrate the wedding of

Miranda and Ferdinand. The happy couple, as everyone noted, were still quite
unable to take their eyes off each other, and were not in the least interested
in Prospero's storytelling! Prospero looked forward to returning to Milan as
its rightful duke after the wedding; a duke who would now pay more attention to his
duties than his library.

Later that night, while everyone slept, Prospero released his faithful Ariel.
No longer would Ariel have to obey his commands, but could fly as free any
sprite might wish. In return, Ariel promised him fair winds and calm
seas for the journey home. Then Prospero discarded his magic cloak, buried
his staff deep in the ground and threw his book of magic out to sea.

After twelve years, Prospero was leaving the enchanted island to Caliban and the
sprites. Prospero's tempest had served its purpose, and his dukedom was restored.
He had no further use for magic. "Now my charms are all o'erthrown, and what
strength I have's mine own," he whispered to the watching eyes of the night.

Hamlet, Prince of Denmark

Long ago in Denmark, the ghost of a man was seen to walk the high, bleak, windswept battlements of Elsinore Castle. He uttered not a word and his footsteps made no sound against the crashing of the surf on the cliffs below. Twice now, the night guards had reported seeing the ghostly figure walk silently along the battlements. He was dressed in full armour and a long cloak whipped the wind behind him. The guards were certain he was not a figment of their imagination. Indeed, they believed he was the spirit of their late king.

The king had been dead for two months and good sense told the guards that his spirit would not return to haunt them, yet they could not shake the idea. Brave as they were, the night soldiers trembled with fear at the unnatural sight. The phantom looked so sad and troubled, but he would not speak, even when a watchman cried out, "What art thou? By heaven, I charge thee, speak!"

Hamlet, Prince of Denmark, son of the late king and heir to his crown, had idolized his father and was completely devastated by his sudden death. His father had been bitten by a serpent while sleeping in his orchard, so his death was unexpected and untimely. The old king had been a great monarch, loved and honoured by all the people of Denmark. Hamlet had thought his mother, Queen Gertrude, also loved his father,

but now he wondered. For while the old king's grave was still freshly dug, she had cast off her widow's garments and married her husband's brother, Claudius, making him the new king. Hamlet hated his mother for feasting and flirting when the meats from his father's funeral were hardly cooled – and he was not the only one to be outraged. Many felt that Queen Gertrude had not shown proper respect to their beloved king.

Hamlet did not mind his uncle stealing his crown, for he was not a youth eager for power, but he thought his uncle was unworthy to rule Denmark. Poor Hamlet – all his old love of life and learning had vanished. His mood grew blacker by the day and he could hardly bring himself to speak to his mother, or her husband, King Claudius.

When Hamlet's friend Horatio told him that his father's ghost, dressed in full armour, had been seen on the battlements, Hamlet listened with foreboding. It seemed to confirm his worst fears. "My father's spirit in arms! All is not well," he muttered.

That night, Hamlet stood watch with Horatio and the guards, hoping and yet dreading to see his father's spirit. The air bit shrewdly at the watchers, even though they were wrapped in thick cloaks. Then, as the hour neared midnight, the ghost appeared as if from nowhere. Silently, he beckoned to Hamlet. Horatio tried to stop Hamlet from following the ghost, begging, "Do not, my lord." But Hamlet did not doubt that this figure was his father's ghost. His face was so pale and so full of anguish that Hamlet could not help but follow him into the shadows of the night, where none could see or hear them.

The ghost spoke of unimagined horrors. The dead king had come to unburden his tortured soul and tell Hamlet that he had not died from a snake bite, as everyone supposed, but had been murdered – by his brother, Claudius.

"'Tis given out that, sleeping in mine orchard, a serpent stung me … but know, thou noble youth, the serpent that did sting thy father's life now wears his crown."

"O my prophetic soul! My uncle!" cried Hamlet.

Although Hamlet despised his uncle, he had not suspected him of murder.

"Oh villain, villain, smiling, damned villain!" he cried.

The ghost swore Hamlet to secrecy, but urged him to take revenge upon Claudius for his death. "If thou didst ever thy dear father love, revenge his foul and most unnatural murder!" he said.

The ghost warned Hamlet not to blame his mother, but to leave her punishment to heaven. And then he whispered, "Fare thee well. Adieu, adieu. Hamlet, remember me." With that, his father's spirit vanished like a wisp of smoke and Hamlet was alone once more.

With bitter tears, Hamlet swore by all the heavenly hosts that he would obey his father's words and revenge his foul murder. This was not a path that Hamlet would have chosen for himself, for he was a gentle prince who dreaded the thought of violence. "The time is out of joint. O cursed spite, that ever I was born to set it right," he sighed, wishing that he could be a carefree student like Horatio.

*T*he days that followed were agony for Hamlet. He could not forget the anguished face of his father's ghost, nor the thought of his murder. He felt unable to trust anyone at court with the ghost's words, and the secret tore holes in his mind. Hamlet's behaviour became wild and unpredictable as he tried to hide his true thoughts. Soon everyone began to notice, including the new king's nosy chamberlain, Polonius.

"Do you know me, my lord?" Polonius asked Hamlet.

"Excellent well; you are a fishmonger," replied Hamlet.

"Not I, my lord."

"Then I would you were so honest a man."

There were times when Hamlet would exaggerate his madness, so that his uncle Claudius and Polonius would not realize that he suspected his father had been murdered. There were also days when even Hamlet could not tell if his madness was real or contrived. He began to be cruel to those he cared for, such as Ophelia, Polonius's sweet daughter, whom he had courted for many months. Hamlet's feelings for her, which had once been so loving and so constant, now appeared to fluctuate between tenderness and scorn.

"I did love you once," he said, as if with no thought for her feelings.

"Indeed my lord, you made me believe so," she said.

"You should not have believed me. I loved you not," he said.

"I was the more deceived," replied Ophelia, her heart heavy with sadness.

*H*amlet felt that everyone at court was spying on him, and every day he grew more miserable and confused. He felt he must obey the words of his father's spirit and yet he had no real proof that his uncle was a murderer. Maybe his father's ghost was the devil in disguise! He began to wonder if it would be better to take his own life rather than kill King Claudius. What should he do? Should he kill himself or his uncle?

"To be, or not to be: that is the question," he said to himself. "Whether 'tis nobler in the mind to suffer the slings and arrows of outrageous fortune, or to take up arms against a sea of troubles, and by opposing end them?"

Hamlet's mother, who was unaware that Claudius had murdered her late husband, thought Hamlet was mad with grief for his father's death and tried to comfort him. "Thou know'st 'tis common: all that lives must die," she said.

Hamlet shrugged her words away. Even if his father's death had been the only cause of his madness, he was in no mood to be comforted by his mother.

Polonius was sure that Hamlet's madness stemmed from his love for Ophelia. Only Claudius feared that there was something more sinister behind Hamlet's behaviour.

Meanwhile, Hamlet's distress grew daily as he watched his mother and his uncle together. "I am but mad north-north-west: when the wind is southerly I know a hawk from a handsaw," he told his friend Guildenstern. Yet sometimes he felt as if the wind, north-north-west or southerly, had blown all his reason away! The days and weeks passed, but still Hamlet could not bring himself to kill his uncle as the phantom had begged. For one thing, his mother and uncle were always together and he could not perform such a vile act in front of his mother. For another, he still had no real proof that his uncle was a murderer.

Then an opportunity arose to test the truth of his ghostly father's words. A famous troupe of actors arrived to perform at Elsinore Castle. Hamlet realized that he could use them to unmask King Claudius. "I'll have these players play something like the murder of my father before mine uncle: I'll observe his looks," he decided.

On the evening of the actors' performance, the court assembled in the great hall of the castle. Torches burned and a great fire was lit. King Claudius and his queen were in high spirits at the thought of the coming entertainment. They sat close together, whispering and laughing. No thought of her recent widowhood seemed to dull the queen's tenderness towards her new husband.

When Prince Hamlet entered with Horatio, to whom he had confided his plan, the queen beckoned to Hamlet. "Come hither, my dear Hamlet, sit by me," she smiled.

Hamlet declined and went to sit near Ophelia, who he began to taunt and tease. When everyone was settled, the actors entered in their tattered costumes and paper crowns and the play began. On Hamlet's orders, the play mimicked the ghost's story of the murder and its consequences. Hamlet stopped taunting Ophelia and watched his uncle's face as a hawk watches his prey. Two actors walked onto the stage, dressed as a king and queen. The king lay down to sleep – and then a third actor entered and poured poison in the sleeping king's ear.

When Claudius saw this, he turned white and abruptly rose from his seat. "Give me some light: away!" he cried. He rushed from the room with the whole court in attendance. Only Hamlet and Horatio were left behind.

"Didst perceive?" asked Hamlet. "Upon the talk of the poisoning?"

"Very well, my lord," said Horatio.

Hamlet no longer doubted his uncle's guilt. "O good Horatio! I'll take the ghost's word for a thousand pound," he said. He knew he could no longer delay his revenge – he must find a way to kill his uncle.

Claudius was now certain that Hamlet suspected him of murdering his father. He asked the queen to call Hamlet to her room and find out what was on his mind. He then ordered Polonius to hide behind the wall hangings so that he could hear all that passed between mother and son;

he knew how much Queen Gertrude loved Hamlet and suspected that she might not tell him everything her son said.

"Behind the arras I'll convey myself," said Polonius, always eager to please the king.

As Polonius strutted off, King Claudius fell to his knees. Suddenly the hideousness of his crime seemed to overcome him. "O! my offence is rank, it smells to heaven," he cried. "It hath the primal eldest curse upon't; a brother's murder!"

As Claudius knelt in prayer with his back towards the open door, Hamlet passed by. He saw the figure of his kneeling uncle and drew his sword. He raised it high above his uncle's back, but then he hesitated. If he took his revenge now while his uncle was at prayer, Claudius's murderous soul might yet go to heaven. Better to kill him when he was not involved in some holy act. "When he is drunk asleep or in his rage, then trip him, that his soul may be as damned and black as hell, whereto it goes," muttered Hamlet, and passed on by.

Hamlet followed the dark and echoing passages of the castle until he reached his mother's room. He had been determined not to lose his temper with her, but he was unable to control his anger when Queen Gertrude spoke of Claudius as his "father".

"Hamlet, thou hast thy father much offended," said the queen.

"Mother, you have my father much offended," replied Hamlet.

"Come, come, you answer with an idle tongue," she said.

"Go, go, you question with a wicked tongue," he retorted.

Their conversation grew more heated. In spite of his ghost father's entreaty not to blame his mother, Hamlet wanted to make her see what she had done and to repent of her wickedness. Queen Gertrude became increasingly agitated as Hamlet raged at her. She tried to run from her room, but Hamlet grabbed hold of her and pulled her back. The queen thought Hamlet was going to kill her. "What wilt thou do? Thou wilt not murder me? Help, help, ho!" she yelled.

From his hiding place behind the tapestry, Polonius also thought that Hamlet was about to murder the queen and called out for the guards. "What, ho! Help, help, help!" he cried.

Hamlet, surprised by this faceless voice, assumed it was his uncle Claudius and plunged his sword again and again through the drapes. "How now, a rat! Dead for a ducat, dead!" he shouted.

He heard a voice gasp, "O, I am slain!" He lifted the hanging … and saw that he had killed Polonius and not Claudius.

Then the ghost appeared to him once more. He urged him to be gentler with Queen Gertrude, but still to avenge his father's death.

"Do you not come your tardy son to chide?" asked Hamlet.

"Do not forget!" replied the ghost.

Hamlet's mother, who could neither see nor hear the ghost, thought Hamlet was talking to himself. "Alas! He's mad," she wept.

Hamlet could hear the guard approaching. He took his leave and hurried away – dragging Polonius with him.

Hamlet hid Polonius's body and for many days refused to tell anyone where it was.

"Now, Hamlet, where's Polonius?" asked Claudius.

"At supper," replied the prince.

"At supper? Where?"

"Not where he eats, but where he is eaten," said Hamlet.

Eventually though, the old man's body was discovered and his murder gave Claudius an excuse to send Hamlet abroad. He arranged for Hamlet to sail to England in the company of his friends Rosencrantz and Guildenstern.

However, England was not far enough away for King Claudius. He would never feel safe while his nephew was still alive. He did not dare kill the young prince on Danish soil where he was known and loved, but in England Hamlet was quite unknown.

There his death would cause no unpleasant ripples for Claudius. He secretly entrusted a letter to Hamlet's friends, asking the English king to execute Hamlet upon his arrival.

But on the journey to England, Hamlet found Claudius's letter. He could not forgive his friends for betraying him, so he forged a new letter, asking the king to kill Rosencrantz and Guildenstern instead of him, and exchanged it for his uncle's note.

The ink was hardly dry when their ship was attacked by pirates. Hamlet leapt aboard the pirate ship to do battle with the rogues, while his cowardly companions deserted him and fled to England – and their deaths. And when the pirates discovered that they had Prince Hamlet on board, they did not murder him, but returned him safely to Denmark, hoping for future favours from the royal household.

When Hamlet reached Elsinore, he was greeted by the news of Ophelia's death. Her heart had been so battered by Hamlet's strange behaviour and her father's violent end that she had become quite deranged. She would wander the castle grounds singing strange and mournful songs and weaving garlands of wild flowers. One day, while garlanding a willow tree, she fell into the brook below and drowned. Hamlet, for all his professed madness, had loved her dearly and he was devastated by her death – as was her brother, Laertes, who blamed Hamlet for both Ophelia's death and his father's.

Laertes hated Hamlet almost as much as King Claudius did. So when Claudius suggested that they should kill Hamlet and make his death look like an accident, Laertes was eager to help. The plan had to be a cunning one to deceive the queen, so they sent a messenger to the prince with an invitation to a friendly fencing match. The messenger said the king had laid a bet that Hamlet would beat Laertes.

"I will win for him if I can; if not, I will gain nothing but my shame and the odd hits," replied Hamlet, who had not for one moment forgotten his promise to the ghost.

The court gathered to witness the battle between Laertes and Hamlet. Laertes made much of choosing his sword, which, unknown to Hamlet, was not a blunt foil like his, but needle-sharp and poisoned. Even a small scratch would bring certain death.

Laertes and Hamlet were well matched and both were elegant fencers. They lunged and parried, their swords clashed, and Hamlet scored several hits. It seemed to all, except the king, that Hamlet would be the winner. But then Laertes suddenly lunged forward. His sword struck Hamlet's arm and drew blood.

Hamlet, realizing that Laertes was fighting with a sharpened blade, let fly his fury. He leapt at Laertes – and in the ensuing scuffle, the swords changed hands and Laertes too was wounded by his own deadly weapon.

"They bleed on both sides," Horatio shouted in horror.

Just at that moment, the queen cried out and collapsed to the floor.

"She swoons to see them bleed," said the king.

"No, no, the drink, the drink. O, my dear Hamlet!" cried the queen. "The drink, the drink; I am poison'd!"

Unwittingly, Queen Gertrude had drunk from a poisoned cup. Hamlet at once suspected his treacherous uncle, and he was right to – the cup had been prepared for him by Claudius, just in case Laertes failed to kill him.

"O villainy! Ho! Let the door be lock'd. Treachery, seek it out!" cried Hamlet.

"It is here, Hamlet," said Laertes, as he too fell dying to the ground.

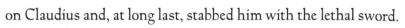

Laertes warned Hamlet that his wound was also mortal, for the sword had been poisoned. Then he confessed his part in Claudius's plot. "The treacherous instrument is in thy hand. Thy mother's poison'd. I can no more. The king, the king's to blame," cried Laertes – and with that, he died.

Hamlet's reaction to his uncle's fresh villainy was both sudden and violent. He leapt on Claudius and, at long last, stabbed him with the lethal sword. "The point envenom'd too? Then, venom, to thy work!" he cried. Then, to make quite sure of his uncle's death, Hamlet forced him to drink from the cup of poison, saying, "Here, thou incestuous, murderous, damned Dane, drink off this potion!"

Hamlet had avenged his father's murder and his mother's murder, too. He staggered and fell to the ground calling out to his dear friend, Horatio. "I am dead, Horatio. Wretched Queen, adieu!"

Horatio ran to Hamlet and held him in his arms. As death drew near, Hamlet saw Horatio reach for the poisoned cup. "Here's yet some liquor left," he said.

Horatio wished to join his friend in death, and would have drunk the last remaining drops of poison, but Hamlet just had the strength to stay his hand.

With his dying breath, Hamlet persuaded Horatio that he must live. "Give me the cup and in this harsh world draw thy breath in pain, to tell my story," he said.

"Goodnight, sweet Prince. And flights of angels sing thee to thy rest," said Horatio as his noble friend slipped away. Moments after Hamlet's death, the Prince of Norway arrived on this terrible scene of murder and revenge. After hearing the true version of events from Horatio, the Prince of Norway ordered his cannons to fire a salute. For everyone who heard the tale knew that had the fates allowed, Hamlet, Prince of Denmark would have been a most royal and noble king.

Antony _and_ Cleopatra

Times were bad for the Roman world. Its borders were constantly under attack from Barbarians, and the money spent on the army to protect them had left many Romans poor and underfed. Rome was ruled by three men: Octavius Caesar, Lepidus and Mark Antony. Caesar and Lepidus did all they could to care for their country from the Senate in Rome – but Mark Antony had vanished to Egypt. He was there, neglecting both his country and his wife, because of the Egyptian queen, Cleopatra. Like Julius Caesar before him, Antony's heart had been captured by Cleopatra's beauty, and he could not bear to leave her.

Most of Antony's Roman friends who had travelled to Egypt with him found it hard to believe that their noble general had fallen for this gypsy queen. She treated their once proud leader like her pet dog, and still he adored her.

One day, into this Egyptian love nest came a messenger from Rome. Antony sent him away without even asking if the message was important. He seemed to have completely forgotten that he was one of Rome's leaders.

"Nay, hear them, Antony," advised Cleopatra. "Hear the ambassadors."

"Fie, wrangling Queen!" complained Antony. But eventually Antony's Roman mind overcame his Egyptian heart and he called the messenger back. The news from Rome was not good. Fulvia, his wife, had

died, and his power in Rome was weakening. Caesar and Lepidus were angry with him for neglecting his duties and another general, Sextus Pompey, was trying to gain power. Antony needed to return to Rome while he still had some followers.

"I must from this enchanting queen break off," he finally decided. "Ten thousand harms, more than the ills I know, my idleness doth hatch."

Cleopatra was furious when she heard that Antony planned to return to Rome. Even the death of Antony's wife failed to please her!

"I am sick and sullen," she said. "O, never was there queen so mightily betray'd."

For once, Antony ignored Cleopatra's pleas and he and his good friend Enobarbus left for Rome.

In Rome there was anger and fear amongst the people, for every day there were fresh uprisings and the noble Antony, whom they had once trusted and admired, was not there to guide them.

Caesar and Lepidus complained bitterly about the length of Antony's stay in Egypt. "From Alexandria this is the news," said Caesar. "He fishes, drinks, and wastes the lamps of night in revel."

"I must not think there are evils enough to darken all his goodness," replied the kinder Lepidus.

Lepidus found it hard to forget what a great leader Antony had once been and decided to prepare a feast to welcome him back to Rome. He hoped that the celebration would lessen Caesar's anger. It did not. From the moment Antony walked into the room, Caesar and Antony were at each other's throats.

Yet Caesar still expressed the wish that, for the sake of Rome and for the noble Antony he had once known, he could repair their friendship somehow. Caesar's friend Agrippa suggested that Antony, who was now a widower, should marry Caesar's sister, Octavia. There was silence. Everyone looked first at Caesar and then at Antony.

"If Cleopatra heard you...!" laughed Caesar.

Antony could not afford to think of Cleopatra at this moment, so he agreed to the plan. The two men shook hands.

"A sister I bequeath you, whom no brother did ever love so dearly," said Caesar. "Let her live to join our kingdoms and our hearts."

Now that the three rulers were united again, they set about retrieving their strength at sea, which Pompey had usurped during Antony's long absence. They sat aboard Pompey's galley, waiting to see if he would agree to their terms.

"You have made me offer of Sicily, Sardinia, and I must rid all the sea of pirates,"

mused Pompey.

"That's our offer," replied the three men in unison.

"Thus we are agreed," smiled Pompey. "We'll feast each other ere we part."

So a peace treaty was signed and Antony, Lepidus and Caesar celebrated with their old friend. Many drinks later, the three leaders returned rather unsteadily to dry land.

"Give's your hand," cried Antony to Pompey as he departed.

"O, Antony!" cried Pompey, delighted to be reunited with his old friend.

Antony felt he had now done everything he could to retain his position in Rome. So he and Octavia, who was now his wife, left for Athens. They had not been there long when some terrible news reached them: Caesar had killed Pompey, imprisoned Lepidus and publicly scorned Antony!

"He hath spoke scantly of me," roared Antony, shocked and unbelieving.

"O my good lord, believe not all," cried Octavia in distress. "Or, if you must believe, stomach not all."

Octavia knew that if this was true it would mean war between her brother and husband. As she was the only person who might be able to prevent it, Octavia left for Rome at once. For the sake of speed, she chose to travel without ceremony,

but her modest arrival infuriated Caesar. He felt Antony had insulted his sister.

"The wife of Antony should have an army for an usher," he ranted, stamping his foot. "But you are come a market-maid to Rome."

"To come thus was I not constrain'd, but did on my free-will," promised Octavia, trying to calm her brother.

If this had been the only insult, Octavia might have succeeded in smoothing her brother's anger, but in Octavia's absence, Antony had gone to visit Cleopatra in Egypt. Caesar was furious and war between the two leaders was now inevitable.

When Cleopatra had heard the news of Antony's marriage to Octavia she had nearly murdered the messenger in a jealous fury. Yet when Antony came back to her, she welcomed him with open arms and he forgot his marriage in an instant. The reunited lovers decided to take up the fight against Caesar at sea, their galleys sailing together.

Enobarbus was appalled at this unwise idea. "Your ships are not well mann'd. Their ships are yare; yours, heavy," he cried.

"By sea, by sea," insisted Antony.

"Most worthy sir, you therein throw away the absolute soldiership you have by land," insisted Enobarbus. For everyone knew Antony was almost unbeatable on land.

However, all Enobarbus's pleas were ignored. Antony only listened to Cleopatra, and she wanted him to take up the battle at sea.

"I have sixty sails, Caesar none better," said Antony, ending the discussion.

Antony and Cleopatra's ships were prepared as well as was possible with their ill-assorted crews, and the lovers left for their ships side by side. Their vessels travelled

across the Ionian Sea towards Caesar's fleet. The lighter Roman ships sped swiftly to meet them. They darted amongst the Egyptian vessels like swallows amidst a herd of elephants, speckling the air with arrows and spears. Antony held firm, shouting encouragement to his beleaguered men.

Then suddenly, without any warning, Cleopatra fled from the battle with all her ships. Antony watched her go in horror – what could this mean? Why was his love deserting him? Forgetting all that was at stake he gave orders for his ship to follow her. If only he had stayed, all might have been well, but now Antony had left his fleet without a leader. Confusion followed, and although some of Antony's ships survived, most were sunk by the Romans.

As soon as Antony's feet touched dry land, he realized what he had done. He was overcome by shame. "Hark, the land bids me tread no more upon't," he wept, "it is ashamed to bear me." He had sacrificed everything for his love of Cleopatra – his honour, his power and his men. He began to feel that the only honourable course was death. "O! Whither hast thou led me, Egypt?" he raged.

"O my lord, my lord! Forgive my fearful sails," returned Cleopatra. "I little thought you would have follow'd."

"Egypt, thou knew'st too well my heart was to thy rudder tied by the strings," Antony said bitterly.

"O! My pardon!" cried the queen, wiping away a tear.

Antony's bitterness quickly melted at the sight of Cleopatra's tears.

"Fall not a tear, I say," he cried opening his arms to her. "One of them rates all that is won and lost. Give me a kiss; even this repays me."

Antony and Cleopatra sent a messenger to Caesar who was encamped outside Alexandria, with terms for peace. The messenger knelt before Caesar.

"Lord of his fortunes he salutes thee and requires to live in Egypt," he said. "Next, Cleopatra does confess thy greatness, submits her to thy might."

"For Antony, I have no ears to his request," said Caesar, coldly. He could not forgive Antony for all that had passed. Antony had insulted both him, his sister and Rome so liberally that Caesar could hardly remember the days when he had thought of Antony as his noble friend. He sent word that he would make peace with Cleopatra only if she drove Antony from Egypt, or had him killed.

To try and encourage Cleopatra to turn against Antony, Caesar sent the message with a cunning and handsome soldier, Thyreus. Thyreus waited until Cleopatra was alone, before conveying Caesar's message. "He knows that you embrace not Antony as you did love, but as you fear'd him," he said, with liquid charm.

Then, as Antony walked into the room, Thyreus took Cleopatra's hand and kissed it, lingering over it for just a moment too long.

Antony immediately suspected her of treachery. "Favours, by Jove that thunders! What art thou, fellow?" Antony yelled. "Moon and stars! Whip him."

Once more, Cleopatra soothed Antony with loving words. Still unable to resist her, his anger cooled. He decided to fight on against Caesar.

"That's my brave lord!" cried Cleopatra.

Much of Antony's army had already drowned or deserted him. Enobarbus had stayed loyal until this moment, but now he could see that anger and love were clouding his friend's judgement. Certain that Antony could no longer defeat Caesar, Enobarbus left to join Caesar's forces. Antony was devastated by this loss. "O! My fortunes have corrupted honest men'" he groaned.

The following day, Antony went into battle with a heavy heart, little caring whether he lived or died. Yet in spite of this, the victory that day went to him, and his spirits rose. "Run one before and let the queen know," he ordered a messenger.

Cleopatra and Antony celebrated all through the night. She called him her "lord of lords" and he called her his "nightingale"! They never doubted for one moment of that starlit night that they would soon secure the final victory.

The next morning the battle moved from land to sea, and Antony manned Cleopatra's galleys with his best troops. Antony was full of hope, and as the day wore on he seemed assured of another victory. Then, without warning, Cleopatra's boats yielded again to Caesar.

"All is lost!" roared Antony. "This foul Egyptian hath betrayed me."

This time Antony's love was totally eclipsed by his anger. He was certain that Cleopatra had betrayed him, and he wanted her to die.

"Why is my lord enrag'd against his love?" appealed Cleopatra.

"Vanish, or I shall give thee thy deserving," he snarled.

Cleopatra ran from the room, calling for her maids. "Help me, my women," she called. "O, he is more than mad!"

Cleopatra took refuge in her tomb and sent word to Antony that she had killed herself.

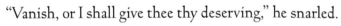

Just as Cleopatra hoped, Antony's rage turned to despair. All was lost now – his honour, his power, his beloved Cleopatra.

"I will o'ertake thee, Cleopatra, and weep for my pardon," Antony cried.

Left without hope, Antony ordered his faithful servant, Eros, to kill him.

"Farewell, great chief. Shall I strike now?" asked Eros.

"Now, Eros," said his master.

"Why, there then; thus do I escape the sorrow..."

To avoid the pain of killing his master, Eros had fallen on his own sword.

Antony was shocked. "Thrice-nobler than myself!" he cried, and threw himself onto his own sword.

As he lay dying, a servant came from Cleopatra to say the queen still lived. Antony begged to be carried to her tomb.

Fearing Caesar's vengeful arrival, Cleopatra would not leave her tomb, so she and her maids hauled Antony over its high walls. Then she held him lovingly in her arms.

"I am dying, Egypt, dying," he whispered. "Now my spirit is going; I can no more."

"Noblest of men, woo't die?" cried Cleopatra in panic. "Has thou no care of me?"

It was no good. With a great cry of anguish, Cleopatra realized that Antony was dead. Wishing to die with him, she fell to the ground.

When Caesar heard that Antony was dead, he was determined to capture Cleopatra alive as a symbol of his victory. He sent one of his officers, Proculeius, to Cleopatra's tomb to prevent the queen from dying along with her lover.

"Her life in Rome would be eternal in our triumph," declared Caesar, almost jumping with delight at the thought.

Proculeius entered the tomb just in time to stop Cleopatra from stabbing herself.

"Where art thou death? Come hither, come!" screamed Cleopatra, furious that Proculeius had prevented her death. Then Caesar himself arrived.

"Our care and pity is so much upon you, that we remain your friend," he promised.

But Cleopatra knew he was secretly plotting to parade her as his prisoner through Rome. She had to act quickly or he would succeed – Caesar was already preparing to return to Rome and Cleopatra was to be sent before him.

First Cleopatra ordered her maids, Charmian and Iras, to fetch her finest robes. "Show me, my women, like a queen," she ordered. "Bring our crown and all." Then she asked them to call for a farmer to deliver a basket of figs.

"Hast thou the pretty worm of Nilus there?" she asked him, when he arrived.

"Truly, I have him," answered the farmer, looking in awe at Egypt's magnificent queen. "But I would not be the party that should desire you to touch him, for his biting is immortal."

Cleopatra waved his worries aside. Once her maids had helped her to dress in all her finery, the queen opened the basket. There, nestled amongst the figs, lay two poisonous asps. Cleopatra lifted them gently, putting one serpent to her breast and one to her arm.

"Dost thou not see my baby at my breast that sucks the nurse asleep?" she said.

"O, break! O, break!" Charmian cried out in distress.

But it was too late. As the asps delivered their venom, Cleopatra thought of Antony. "O Antony!" she whispered, as though with her dying breath she fell into his arms.

By their deaths, Antony and Cleopatra had robbed Caesar of his triumph. Yet Antony had once been the noblest of Roman generals, and in spite of all their quarrels, Caesar mourned for him. He gave orders that the bodies of Charmian and Iras, who had poisoned themselves, be removed from the monument. Then his army attended Antony and Cleopatra's funeral with full solemnity, placing the two lovers together in the queen's tomb so they would stay in death as they had in life, side by side.

Twelfth Night
or *What You Will*

Orsino, Duke of Illyria, was lying on a couch, listening to his lute player's doleful ballads while dreaming of the countess Olivia. "If music be the food of love, play on, give me excess of it," he sighed. The countess, who lived close by, consumed the duke's thoughts both day and night. He was quite hopelessly in love with her. Unfortunately for Orsino, Olivia was in mourning for her dead brother and had sworn to allow no men into her house, or her thoughts, for seven years.

"Will you go hunt, my lord?" asked Orsino's servant Curio, hoping to distract his lovesick master and get away from the lute player's serenading.

"O, when mine eyes did see Olivia first, methought she purg'd the air of pestilence!" sighed Orsino.

Curio threw up his arms in despair – truly, if his master preferred the countess to hunting, he was beyond saving!

The previous night, there had been a terrible storm over Illyria, and although the duke knew nothing of it, a ship had been wrecked on the rocky coast below his castle. One of the few survivors was a gentlewoman named Viola who had been aboard the vessel with her twin brother, Sebastian. Sebastian had vanished in the waves and Viola feared he was drowned. Poor Viola was now alone in the world, with no money. So the ship's captain advised her to dress as a man and seek work at the court of Illyria's ruler, Duke Orsino.

Dressed in doublet and hose, Viola made a convincing young man. She could sing mournful love ballads very beautifully, so Orsino was delighted to employ her as his page. Over the following days, he found his new page gentle and soothing to his lovesick heart, and he soon came to trust Viola above all his other servants. "I have unclasp'd to thee the book even of my secret soul," he sighed to Viola, after telling her of his love for the countess Olivia.

Orsino asked his new page to try and woo Olivia for him as the countess had refused to let him, or any of his other servants, into her house. Viola was most reluctant to take on the task for since arriving at the castle she had gradually fallen in love with Orsino herself.

"Say I do speak with her, my lord, what then?" asked Viola.

"O, then unfold the passion of my love," cried the duke.

"I'll do my best to woo your lady," Viola assured him.

Yet what she really wished to do was to throw off her page's attire, put on a beautiful dress and capture Orsino's heart for herself!

As Olivia would not allow men into her house, Viola was turned away on her first visit. But as she had promised Orsino she would deliver his message, she refused to move from the gate. Even when Olivia's rude steward, Malvolio, offered a dozen excuses why Olivia would not see her, Viola stood her ground. Finally Malvolio returned to Olivia, his feathers thoroughly ruffled.

"Madam, yond young fellow swears he will speak with you," he declared. "I told him you were sick … I told him you were asleep. What is to be said to him, lady?"

"What kind o' man is he?" asked Olivia.

"He is very well favoured and he speaks very shrewishly," grumbled Malvolio.

"Let him approach," said Olivia, who was growing bored of her own company.

As soon as the handsome young page entered Olivia's room, her heart lurched. She listened enraptured as Viola, on behalf of her master, began to praise her.

"Most radiant, exquisite, and unmatchable beauty," the page began.

Eventually Olivia felt obliged to try and silence this outpouring, since, as she explained to Viola, she did not love Orsino and never would.

"I pray you, keep it in. I cannot love him. Let him send no more," cried Olivia. "Unless, perchance you come to me again..." For Orsino's page had flattered Olivia

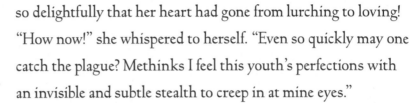

so delightfully that her heart had gone from lurching to loving!

"How now!" she whispered to herself. "Even so quickly may one catch the plague? Methinks I feel this youth's perfections with an invisible and subtle stealth to creep in at mine eyes."

Viola left the countess with a heavy heart. Olivia had rejected the very thought of loving Orsino and her curt dismissal was likely to make her master weep. As Viola wandered slowly home, pondering how best to break this news to the duke, Malvolio came puffing up behind her.

"Were not you even now with the countess Olivia?" he gasped.

"Even now, sir," replied the page.

"She returns this ring to you, sir," said Malvolio.

Viola knew at once that the ring was not hers, but a love token from Olivia. She was mortified to think that Olivia had believed in her page's costume and, thinking her a man, had fallen in love with her. She wished she could reveal her disguise, but then she would be without work or money.

Viola tried to refuse the ring, but peevish Malvolio just threw it at her feet and walked off.

"Poor lady, she were better love a dream," sighed Viola, as she stooped to pick up the beautiful ring. "Disguise I see thou art a wickedness."

As much as she would have liked to, Viola could think of no way of untangling this confusion without revealing her true identity.

That night, the countess Olivia went to bed early, dreaming not of Orsino but his page. However, her maid, Maria, her jester, Feste, her uncle, Sir Toby Belch, and his friend, Sir Andrew Aguecheek, all stayed up late, revelling and drinking. Sir Toby hoped that Sir Andrew might marry Olivia, for although he was much older than her, he was very rich and kept Sir Toby well supplied with wine.

As the night wore on, they reached that stage when voices begin to slur into song and every note seems perfectly pitched.

"O mistress mine, where are you roaming? O! Stay and hear; your true love's coming," sang the jester as he swayed back and forth.

"A mellifluous voice, as I am true knight," declared Sir Andrew.

"A contagious breath," said Sir Toby, pouring more wine.

"My masters are you mad?" cried Malvolio, bursting into the room. "Have you no wit, manners nor honesty but to gabble like tinkers at this time of night?"

Sir Toby protested that a servant had no right to talk to him in such a way, but Malvolio would have none of it. He ended their revelry and packed them all off to bed.

The next day, the angry revellers decided to pay Malvolio back for spoiling their fun, and came up with the perfect plan. As Malvolio walked about the garden, they dropped a letter in his path which Maria had written in Olivia's handwriting. Just as the tricksters hoped, Malvolio picked up the letter from the ground. "By my life," he cried, "this is my lady's hand!"

As he started to read, his excitement grew, for it was a love letter! As he read on, he became convinced that he was "the unknown beloved" to whom the letter was addressed! It seemed that his mistress loved him; she commanded him to always wear cross-gartered yellow stockings and always smile in her presence. "Thy smiles become thee well," he read.

"Jove I thank thee," cried the duped steward, kissing the letter. "I will smile; I will do everything that thou wilt have me."

Poor Malvolio believed that Olivia might marry him. He rushed to his room to change his stockings and then he sought Olivia out. Smiling as broadly as he was able, he started to strut up and down in front of her, showing off his yellow cross-gartered stockings. Olivia, who knew nothing of the letter, thought he had gone mad.

"Wilt thou go to bed, Malvolio?" she asked kindly.

"To bed, ay sweetheart; and I'll come to thee," said Malvolio, winking and kissing his hand.

"God comfort thee," cried Olivia, growing more concerned. "Why dost thou smile and kiss thy hand so oft?"

Malvolio quoted whole sentences from the letter, but still Olivia looked bewildered. Finally, she gave orders that he be locked up in a dark room till he had recovered his senses. Poor Malvolio was carried off kicking and shouting at such injustice.

Later that day, Viola arrived at Olivia's home, still acting as Orsino's page. She bowed deeply to Olivia and said that she had come to tell her of Orsino's love.

Again Olivia refused to listen to Orsino's suit, rejecting him entirely. The only person Olivia wanted to wed was Orsino's page, but every time she tried to woo the page, the page talked of Orsino.

"I love thee so," Olivia eventually burst out, abandoning all pretence of pride. Viola was horrified and didn't know how to answer Olivia.

"I am not what I am," Viola insisted at last. She tried to rush away, and swore to herself that she would never again be her master's messenger.

"Yet come again!" cried Olivia, as Viola finally managed to flee from the house.

Sir Andrew overheard this exchange. He, like Duke Orsino, had been rejected by Olivia on countless occasions. He realized that Olivia was in love with the duke's page and he went off angrily to complain to Sir Toby.

"Marry, I saw your niece do more favours to the count's serving-man than ever she bestowed upon me," he grumbled.

Sir Toby was most concerned; if Sir Andrew gave up trying to court his niece, he might lose his supply of wine! He encouraged Sir Andrew to challenge this new rival to a duel. "Hurt him in eleven places: my niece shall take note of it," he assured his friend.

Meanwhile Viola's twin, Sebastian, hadn't drowned after all. He had been washed up on the shore some way down the coast and had been rescued by a sea captain called Antonio, an old enemy of Orsino's. Like Viola, he thought his twin was dead, and he mourned her deeply. To distract him, Antonio persuaded him to go and explore the town. Antonio was nervous because if he was discovered by the duke's men he would be arrested, so he went to look for discreet lodgings while Sebastian toured the local sights. Antonio, knowing that Sebastian had no money, lent him his purse and arranged to meet him later at a certain inn. Antonio had forgotten that he would need his purse to secure their lodgings, so he soon found himself chasing after Sebastian, who seemed to have vanished down a maze of narrow streets.

Eventually he found Sebastian and was astonished to see that he was fighting! Little did Antonio realize this was Sebastian's twin, Viola, duelling with Sir Andrew. Antonio rushed to "Sebastian's" defence.

"If this young gentleman have done offence, I take the fault on me," he declared, gallantly.

"You, sir! Why, what are you?" cried Sir Toby.

As fate would have it, some soldiers were standing close by. Before the argument could be settled, they recognized Antonio as the duke's enemy and arrested him.

"Antonio, I arrest thee at the suit of Count Orsino," said the officer.

"You do mistake me, sir," lied Antonio.

"No, sir, no jot: I know your favour well," returned the officer.

Antonio asked "Sebastian" to return his purse so that he could buy his freedom. Viola, who had never seen Antonio before, was astonished at his request and refused.

"What money, sir?" she asked, in all innocence.

Antonio could not believe that the youth he had dragged from the surf and befriended should repay his kindness in this way.

"Thou hast, Sebastian, done good feature shame," he ranted at Viola in a fury, as the soldiers dragged him away.

Viola stood thunderstruck. This man had used Sebastian's name! He must know her brother, and her brother must still be alive! In a whirl of excitement, Viola fled back up the hill to Duke Orsino's house.

Sir Andrew, who had stood by and watched all this, felt cheated of his duel. So he and Toby chased Viola – but they ended up catching Sebastian! Sebastian had carried on sightseeing, unaware of all the drama. He was innocently wandering past Olivia's home, admiring its fine design, when Sir Andrew marched up to him and slapped him in the face!

"Now, sir, have I met you again? There's for you," Sir Andrew cried.

"Why, there's for thee, and there, and there!" yelled Sebastian, beating Sir Andrew as hard as he could. "Are all the people mad?"

Seeing Sir Andrew sink to his knees, Sir Toby grabbed hold of
Sebastian and tried to calm him.

"Come on sir, hold," he pleaded.

All the men were in a fury now, and within minutes, all had drawn their swords.
They were making such a racket that Olivia rushed from her house to see what the
commotion was about.

"Hold, Toby! On thy life I charge thee, hold!" she cried in horror, thinking that
Sir Toby was about to run his sword through her beloved. She chased her uncle and Sir
Andrew into the house and then turned to the man she believed to be Orsino's page.
She begged him not to go, but to stay and hear about her love for him. Sebastian couldn't
make out if he was in a dream or if everyone had indeed gone mad. He guessed that
Olivia loved him through some mistake, but he had no desire to resist her advances!

"If it be thus to dream, still let me sleep," he declared, happily.

"Would thou'dst be ruled by me!" smiled Olivia.

"Madam, I will," replied Sebastian, too bemused to argue.

"O say so, and so be!" exclaimed Olivia.

Olivia couldn't believe that her page might return her love at last.
So, rather than let the moment pass and risk losing him again, Olivia
rushed Sebastian to the town church to be married.

After the wedding, the confused but happy Sebastian left his new bride while he
went in search of Antonio to return his purse. At the same time, Duke Orsino,
who knew nothing of the wedding, set out with Viola to beg the countess Olivia
to marry him! On their way to Olivia's house, they met Antonio
being marched to jail by two officers. Viola pointed him out to
the duke as the gentleman who had rescued her from a duel.
But Antonio pointed at Viola and cried, "That most ingrateful
boy there by your side denied me mine own purse!"

Viola denied all knowledge of the purse and the duke dismissed Antonio's claim. Then Olivia appeared and all else flew from Duke Orsino's thoughts.

"Here comes the countess," he gasped, "now heaven walks on earth!"

Olivia ignored the duke, for she only had eyes for his page, who she kept referring to as her "husband"! This made both duke and page gasp.

"Her husband, sirrah!" shouted the duke in a fury. "O, thou dissembling cub!"

The duke was furious to think that his trusted page had stolen his countess. He might have set about Viola if Sir Toby and Sir Andrew hadn't hobbled up, both moaning loudly and shaking their fists at Viola.

"He has broke my head across, and has given Sir Toby a bloody coxcomb too," complained Sir Andrew.

"Why do you speak to me? I never hurt you," swore Viola.

Then, as if by magic, another Viola was seen wandering up the street towards them! Everyone fell silent and everyone stared.

"One face, one voice, one habit, and two persons," uttered the duke in confusion.

"How have you made division of yourself?" wondered Antonio. "An apple cleft in two is not more twin than these two creatures."

Then, as Viola embraced Sebastian, the confusion began to clear – the page was not a boy at all, but this young man's sister!

"Most wonderful!" exclaimed Olivia, throwing her arms around Sebastian. For she realized with relief that Sebastian was her true husband and not the dissembling Viola.

Duke Orsino was stunned and looked at his page in utter astonishment. He might have been furious, but instead he remembered Viola's tenderness towards him and realized that she must have loved him from the first. So he gave up his wasted love for Olivia and offered his heart to Viola, who felt close to fainting with happiness.

"Give me thy hand; and let me see thee in thy woman's weeds," smiled her duke.

In high good humour, the duke pardoned Antonio for his past misdeeds and Sebastian gave him his purse back. Olivia wanted everyone to share in her happiness, so called for her steward to be released.

"Madam," Malvolio cried. "You have done me wrong. Notorious wrong."

"Have I, Malvolio? No," insisted Olivia. But no amount of explaining would convince Malvolio that his mistress was not part of the plot against him.

"Alas, poor fool, how have they baffled thee!" sighed Olivia.

"I'll be revenged on the whole pack of you!" Malvolio cried, and he marched off, his cross-gartered yellow stockings flashing through the evening gloom.

Not even Malvolio's furious departure could cast a shadow over the rest of the company. As Olivia's jester, Feste, began to sing a song of celebration, everyone except Malvolio linked arms in love and friendship. The terrible shipwreck on Illyria's shores had turned out to have a silver lining.

A great while ago the world begun,
With a hey, ho, the wind and the rain;
But that's all one, our play is done,
And we'll strive to please you every day.

The Tragedy of King Richard III

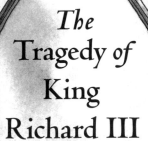

*T*he streets of London were rank with the smell of death and sewage. The hunchbacked Richard, Duke of Gloucester, revelled in the stench. With his hand always close to his dagger and his thoughts always on dark deeds, one of his few delights was watching his own deformed shadow creep across the city's walls. As he prowled through the city, he muttered lonely, bitter words – words that would have made any eavesdropper shiver with fear: "Since I cannot prove a lover to entertain these fair well-spoken days, I am determined to prove a villain!"

The year was 1483 and Richard's brother, King Edward IV, lay close to death. His son, the Prince of Wales, would inherit the crown even though he was still a child. As the boy's uncle, Richard was "Lord Protector" of the realm and entrusted with the prince's care. But this was not enough for the ambitious hunchback – Richard wanted the crown for himself. And he was ready to use any means to get it, however foul.

Richard realized that as king he would need to have a well-born wife. He would have to become a lover after all. "I'll marry Warwick's youngest daughter, Anne," he mused. Warwick was the late King Henry VI and Richard had murdered him, along with his son – but this seemed to make the challenge of winning Anne all the more delightful to Richard's twisted mind.

The following day, Richard lurked in the shadows of another street – the street where Anne's father's coffin would pass. As the funeral cortege drew close, Richard

jumped from the shadows with his cloak flying out behind him, like a black fiend of hell. "Stay, you that bear the corpse, and set it down," he cried.

Anne was shaken out of her misery. She knew at once that this fearful intruder was Richard. The bearers stumbled to a halt. "What!" cried Anne. "Do you tremble? Are you all afraid?" Yet how could she blame the bearers? It was only anger that kept her from trembling with fear. "Foul devil," she screamed at Richard, "for God's sake hence, and trouble us not."

"Lady, you know no rules of charity," smiled Richard.

"Out of my sight! Thou dost infect mine eyes," cried Anne, outraged that her father's killer should dare to come so close to his coffin.

"Thine eyes, sweet lady, have infected mine. If thy revengeful heart cannot forgive,

lo, here I lend thee this sharp-pointed sword," said Richard, thrusting his sword into Anne's hand.

Anne took the sword. How easy it would be to avenge her father's and brother's deaths! Richard tore aside his cloak and exposed his chest. She lifted the sword to strike – but then let it fall. "Though I wish thy death, I will not be the executioner," she said.

Richard smiled in triumph. He was winning. She would be his wife. "I'll have her, but I will not keep her long!" he thought to himself.

"Vouchsafe to wear this ring," he smarmed, taking a ring from his own finger.

"To take is not to give," replied Anne, confused at this turn of events.

Then the bearers picked up the coffin and the procession moved forwards, leaving a dark shadow on the wall behind them.

But if Richard were to be king, he didn't just need a noble wife – he also needed to be rid of his elder brother, the popular Duke of Clarence. So he persuaded the weakening King Edward to imprison Clarence as a traitor in the Tower of London.

As the confused duke was marched to the tower by two guards, Richard limped up
to his brother and pretended to comfort him. Poor Clarence trusted him to secure
his release. But then Richard vanished back into the gloom, muttering, "Simple, plain
Clarence! I do love thee so, that I will shortly send thy soul to heaven!"

Richard wasted no time in dispatching his brother – he hired a pair of assassins to
murder Clarence in his cell. When the guard let them in, Clarence was in a deep sleep,
haunted by nightmares of drowning. The two murderers looked down at the duke.

"Shall we stab him as he sleeps?" asked one.

"No; he'll say 'twas done cowardly when he wakes," laughed the other, kicking
Clarence awake.

Clarence saw at once what the two men meant to do, and he leapt from his bed
in terror. "I will send you to my brother Gloucester, who shall reward you better

for my life!" he cried in panic.

"Your brother Gloucester hates you," they laughed.

Even then, Clarence could not believe Richard could be so evil
and deceiving. But he had no time to dwell on these thoughts, for
as he fell to his knees to beg for mercy a dagger entered his back.

Again and again the murderer stabbed him – but still Clarence did not die.

"If all this will not do, I'll drown you in the malmsey-butt within," shouted the
desperate villain. And lifting Clarence up, he plunged him
head first into a barrel of wine. He held Clarence's head
under the red liquid until he ceased to struggle and no
more bubbles rose to the surface. Poor Clarence died by
drowning, just as his dream had foretold.

Richard was well pleased with the murder of Clarence, and thought he had judged the timing of it well, as King Edward died shortly afterwards. The king's grieving widow, Queen Elizabeth, was well aware of Richard's ruthless ambition, and she feared for her family; her sons, the two little princes, were all that stood between him and the crown. So she quickly sent her brothers to Ludlow to bring her eldest son, the Prince of Wales, to London for his coronation.

When Richard's friend, the Duke of Buckingham, heard that the prince was coming to London, his mind worked quickly. He was almost as sly as Richard himself – he hoped to be rewarded well if Richard became king, and he did not want the Prince of Wales to be crowned instead.

"My lord, whoever journeys to the prince, for God's sake let not us two stay at home," he whispered to Richard.

"My other self, my counsel's consistory, my oracle, my prophet!" smiled Richard. "Towards Ludlow then, for we'll not stay behind."

So Richard and the Duke of Buckingham hastened to Ludlow and took the young prince into their own charge. When the queen's brothers arrived, Richard had them executed on the trumped-up charge of plotting to murder the Duke of Clarence.

Elizabeth was more scared than ever when she heard that Richard had taken her eldest son and executed her brothers. "Ah me! I see the ruin of our house! The tiger hath seized the gentle hind," she cried, clutching her youngest son to her. "Come, come, my boy, we will to sanctuary." So she fled to the abbey to seek holy sanctuary with the young Duke of York.

Perhaps she should have guessed that even holy sanctuary had no meaning for ruthless Richard. He ordered the little Duke of York to be taken from his mother and had the two young princes locked in the Tower of London, safely out of his way.

The youngest prince wept at the thought of seeing his dead Uncle Clarence's ghost. "I shall not sleep in quiet at the Tower," he cried. The innocent young prince did not realize he had more reason to fear his living uncle than a dead one.

By now, Hastings, the Lord Chamberlain, had guessed Richard's plans. "I'll have this crown of mine cut from my shoulders before I'll see the crown so foul misplac'd," he declared angrily. But scheming Richard was determined not to let anyone stand in his way. So, in front of Hastings, he falsely accused Queen Elizabeth of witchcraft, the penalty for which was death.

"Look how I am bewitch'd," he demanded of Hastings, rolling up his sleeve and revealing a withered arm. "Behold mine arm is like a blasted sapling."

But Hastings could not bring himself to believe that the queen was guilty of witchcraft.

Richard realized that Hastings would never sign the queen's death warrant. "Thou protector of this damned strumpet!" he shouted. "Thou art a traitor – off with his head!"

"O bloody Richard! Miserable England!" cried Hastings in despair. "Come, lead me to the block."

Next, Richard told the faithful Buckingham to spread rumours that the princes had been born out of wedlock.

"Doubt not my lord, I'll play the orator," promised Buckingham. He went about passing the rumour from person to person. It spread to all the dukes and lords at court, then on through the streets of London. Eventually, the people became so unsettled that they began to call for Richard to be king.

"Good my lord; your citizens entreat you," declared the Mayor of London.

"Refuse not, mighty lord, this proffer'd love," grinned Buckingham.

"Alas, why would you heap those cares on me? I am unfit for state and majesty," said Richard, as innocently as he was able. "I do beseech you, take it not amiss, I cannot nor I will not yield to you."

Of course, the citizens' cries were what Richard had been hoping for. His heart was dancing with delight and his head itched to feel the weight of the crown – it was all he could do not to crow with triumph!

At last, the day came when he was crowned King Richard III of England. He sat upon the throne, with the crown on his head … but instead of feeling regal and all-powerful, doubt gnawed at his insides. How secure was he on the throne? Were there already plots against him? He turned to Buckingham for some reassurance.

"Ha! Am I king?" he questioned. "'Tis so: but Edward lives."

"True, noble Prince," replied Buckingham, nervously.

"Shall I be plain? I wish the bastards dead; and I would have it suddenly performed."

Buckingham tried to look unmoved, but could not cover his sharp intake of breath. Thus far he had supported Richard, but killing two young children was more than he could stomach. Yet while the little princes lived, Richard would feel insecure. "Give me some little breath, some pause, dear lord," pleaded Buckingham, playing for time.

But Richard was not going to wait for anyone. He ignored Buckingham and paid an assassin to smother the boys as they slept. Then he ordered their bodies to be buried before his evil deed was discovered.

When Buckingham tried to claim a long-promised earldom, he learned the cost of hesitating to follow the king's commands.

"My lord, I claim the gift, my due by promise," Buckingham said.

"I am not in the giving vein today," came Richard's icy reply, and he swept out of the room, his royal robes dragging behind him.

Buckingham realized at once that Richard had turned against him. His hesitation over the murder of the young princes had put his own life in danger. "Made I him king for this?" he asked himself as he watched the hunched shadow retreat along the passage. "O, let me think on Hastings, and be gone, while my fearful head is on."

So Buckingham fled to raise an army and join the growing forces against the king. Yet Richard still believed he could secure the throne if he got rid of Anne and married the dead princes' sister, Elizabeth. But he suspected that Henry, Earl of Richmond also wanted to marry Elizabeth and become king. He would have to act fast and woo Elizabeth before Richmond. But he had no time, for news came that Richmond was already marching against him.

Richmond was a powerful adversary and many of those who had fled Richard's court had gone to join forces with him. Richard knew he must fight him or lose the crown. He rallied his army and set out for Wales. Along the way he was met by a messenger with news of Buckingham. Expecting more bad tidings, Richard struck the messenger in a fury. The poor messenger fell to the ground, protesting that he had brought good news: Buckingham's army had been caught in a flood, his soldiers had scattered and Buckingham himself was captured. Suddenly, Richard was all smiles. He threw his purse at the poor messenger.

"I cry thee mercy," said Richard. "There is my purse, to cure that blow of thine."

The two great armies of Richard and Richmond met on Bosworth Field. The night before the battle began, both the king and Richmond dreamed of Richard's victims. One by one, the spectres wished Richard ill and the Earl of Richmond well.

"Despair and die!" they cried to Richard, who tossed and cried out in his sleep. "Live, and flourish! Awake, and win the day!" they cried to Richmond.

The day dawned sunless and cold. As the trumpets sounded, the soldiers charged, and the noise of battle resounded around the field. Richard fought bravely, but his side suffered heavy losses. Then his own horse was slain beneath him. "A horse! A horse! My kingdom for a horse!" he cried, as the great beast fell.

In the chaos of battle there was no horse to be found, so Richard fought on foot. Finally, he found himself face to face with Richmond. The power of the crown was no use to the raging hunchback now. It was clear to all that he was no match for the earl. With one victorious stroke, Richmond slew him.

"God and your arms be praised, victorious friends," cried Richmond. "The day is ours, the bloody dog is dead!"

Richard III's short and blood-stained reign was over. Few mourned its passing and many celebrated the crowning of Richmond as King Henry VII. Henry then married the princes' sister, Elizabeth – uniting her House of York with his House of Lancaster, to bring peace and prosperous days to England.

The Merchant of Venice

Long ago in Venice, there lived a merchant named Antonio. He was honest and generous and well loved by his friends. When Antonio's luck was in, and his ships arrived safely at port with their rich cargo, he would lend his money to whoever asked and expect no interest.

Antonio was particularly generous to his good friend Bassanio. Bassanio was a young man of noble birth, but he was very poor and had often borrowed from Antonio. Now Bassanio had decided that the time had come to clear his debts once and for all.

"To you, Antonio, I owe the most, in money and in love," he declared.

"My purse, my person, my extremest means, lie all unlocked to your occasions," promised the good-hearted merchant.

"In Belmont is a lady richly left," said Bassanio. "And she is fair, fairer than that word."

Gradually it unfolded that Bassanio was in love with Portia, a rich heiress who lived in Belmont, near Venice. Bassanio thought his love might be returned, and if it was, he would never have to borrow money again. The problem was that to travel to Portia's estate and to court her in a fitting manner, Bassanio needed three thousand ducats!

"Thou know'st that all my fortunes are at sea. Neither have I money nor commodity to raise a present sum," said Antonio. But he decided to see if he could borrow money against his good name until his ships arrived.

Antonio and Bassanio went to the Rialto, where the money lenders gathered. They asked Shylock, a Jew, to lend them the money and were surprised when he agreed – it was well known that Shylock hated Antonio. He hated him because Antonio stole his customers by lending money without interest, and also because Antonio treated him with scorn. Antonio willingly admitted this – but Bassanio needed money. For him, Antonio was willing to overlook his dislike of Shylock.

"Well, Shylock, shall we be beholding to you?" asked Antonio with no great warmth.

"You call me misbeliever, cut-throat dog, and spit upon my Jewish gaberdine," said Shylock. "Well then, it now appears you need my help."

"If thou wilt lend this money, lend it not as to thy friends, but lend it rather to thine enemy," said Antonio.

Strangely, Shylock agreed to lend the money to Antonio without interest. Shylock suggested another bond: if the money was not returned in three months, as Antonio promised it would be, he must pay with a pound of his flesh. "An equal pound, to be cut off and taken in what part of your body pleaseth me," said Shylock.

This was just by way of a jest, Shylock said, but it didn't seem so to Bassanio. "You shall not seal to such a bond for me!" he cried, horrified.

"Why, fear not, man," Antonio reassured him. "I will not forfeit it. Within these two months, I do expect return of thrice three times the value of this bond."

So Antonio rashly agreed. He went with Shylock to the notary and signed the bond.

With the money in his purse, Bassanio prepared for his visit to Portia. He acquired a small retinue of servants and bought himself some richly embroidered garments, befitting a young man about to woo his love.

His friend Gratiano begged to accompany him. "You must not deny me," Gratiano said. Bassanio laughingly agreed, but he warned his friend not to be too wild or loud in case it set Portia against his suit. For many fine nobles had tried to win the lady for their wife, but none had succeeded.

This was partly because Portia did not like any of them, and partly because of her father. Before he had died, Portia's father had made three caskets with a riddle inscribed on each one. One casket was made of gold, and read: "Who chooseth me shall gain what many men desire." Another was made of silver, and read: "Who chooseth me shall get as much as he deserves." The last one was made of lead, and read: "Who chooseth me must give and hazard all he hath." Portia's father had decreed that the first suitor to pick the casket that contained a portrait of his daughter would win her hand.

"By my troth, Nerissa, my little body is aweary of this great world," sighed Portia to her maid, after yet another man had tried and failed to choose the correct casket.

At first the arrival of another suitor did not excite Portia, but when she heard it was Bassanio her mood changed. Bassanio had been at Belmont for just a few days when it became obvious to all that he and Portia loved each other.

Bassanio was eager to know his fate and try his hand at choosing the casket, but Portia had seen many other suitors fail. "I pray you, tarry: pause a day or two before you hazard," she begged. "For, in choosing wrong I lose your company."

"Let me choose; for as I am I live upon the rack," said Bassanio, who already found it impossible to imagine his future without Portia.

"Away then! I am locked in one of them. If you do love me, you will find me out," said Portia, sounding more certain than she felt.

So the caskets were brought and laid before Bassanio. Portia, Nerissa and Gratiano watched him nervously. Gold, silver, or lead? Which should Bassanio choose?

He stared at the caskets long and hard. "So may the outward shows be least themselves: the world is still deceived with ornament," Bassanio said to himself. "Therefore, thou gaudy gold, I will none of thee. Nor none of thee," he said, looking at the silver casket. "But thou, thou meagre lead, here choose I: joy be the consequence!"

With a shaking hand, he turned the key in the lead casket … and found his true love's portrait! Everyone clapped their hands in delight. Portia and Bassanio hugged each other with relief. When Bassanio  confessed that he had many debts and no wealth of his own, Portia put his mind at rest, promising that she had wealth enough for both of them.

"This house, these servants, and this same myself are yours, my lord. I give them with this ring; which when you part from, lose, or give away, let it presage the ruin of your love," said Portia, handing Bassanio a ring.

Bassanio took it gratefully and swore he would never part with it. Then, to everyone's surprise and delight, Nerissa and Gratiano announced that they too had fallen in love. So Nerissa gave Gratiano a ring and, just as Bassanio had done, Gratiano promised never to part with this token of Nerissa's love.

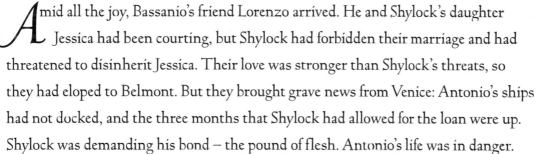

Amid all the joy, Bassanio's friend Lorenzo arrived. He and Shylock's daughter Jessica had been courting, but Shylock had forbidden their marriage and had threatened to disinherit Jessica. Their love was stronger than Shylock's threats, so they had eloped to Belmont. But they brought grave news from Venice: Antonio's ships had not docked, and the three months that Shylock had allowed for the loan were up. Shylock was demanding his bond – the pound of flesh. Antonio's life was in danger.

"What sum owes he the Jew?" asked Portia.

"For me, three thousand ducats," said Bassanio in great distress.

"What, no more? You shall have gold to pay the petty debt twenty times over," said Portia, trying to comfort Bassanio.

So that Bassanio would have easy access to Portia's money, the couples decided to marry immediately. Then Bassanio and Gratiano left for Venice to try to save Antonio.

"Since I have your good leave to go away, I will make haste; but, till I come again, no bed shall be guilty of my stay," promised Bassanio, kissing his new wife.

Left behind, Portia wondered how she could help Bassanio's friend, for she hated to see her husband in distress. She decided to write to her cousin, the learned lawyer Doctor Bellario. She asked him to send lawyers' clothes and books about the law to Venice. Then Portia asked Lorenzo and Jessica to look after her house, and said she and Nerissa would move into the local monastery until their husbands returned.

"Come on, Nerissa: I have work in hand that you yet know not of. We'll see our husbands before they think of us," said Portia, trying to hurry her maid.

"Shall they see us?" asked Nerissa.

"They shall, Nerissa," smiled her mistress with a twinkle in her eye.

A few days later, Shylock brought his case against Antonio to the duke's court in Venice. Bassanio was there with Portia's money, but because the three months had expired, Shylock refused to take the larger sum Bassanio offered. He wanted revenge on his old enemy and was insisting on his pound of Antonio's flesh.

"How shalt thou hope for mercy, rendering none?" asked the duke.

"What judgement shall I dread, doing no wrong?" replied Shylock. "The pound of flesh, which I demand of him, is dearly bought; 'tis mine and I will have it."

The whole court was horrified, but Shylock would not relent. "He hath disgraced me, laughed at my losses, mocked at my gains: and what's his reason? I am a Jew. Hath not a Jew eyes? Hath not a Jew hands, organs, dimensions, senses, affections, passions? If you prick us, do we not bleed? If you tickle us, do we not laugh? If you poison us, do we not die? And if you wrong us, shall we not revenge?"

So the duke sent for an expert, Doctor Bellario, for advice. The lawyer was unwell but sent in his place a promising pupil and his clerk. Those present at court felt little confidence in this youth, for he looked too young to wield much wisdom. The young lawyer soon confirmed their views by announcing that the law stood against Antonio. Shylock was delighted and began to sharpen his knife.

"Why dost thou whet thy knife so earnestly?" cried out Bassanio.

"To cut the forfeiture from the bankrupt there," said Shylock.

The lawyer then asked Shylock to be merciful and to drop the charge. "The quality of mercy is not strain'd, it droppeth as the gentle rain from heaven upon the place beneath," explained the lawyer. "It is twice bless'd; it blesseth him that gives and him that takes."

Yet it seemed that Shylock was without mercy. "I crave the law," he cried.

"I am arm'd and well prepar'd," said Antonio, thinking he was about to die.

The lawyer stopped Shylock's eager hand. He warned Shylock that the bond allowed him to take a pound of flesh exactly. "Shed thou no blood, nor cut thou less, nor more, but just a pound of flesh," warned the lawyer, calling for scales to be brought.

If Shylock spilled one drop of blood, or cut one hair's weight over the pound, he would break the law. Then he risked death or the loss of his estate. It seemed this lawyer had more wisdom than the court had thought. Shylock dropped his knife. He decided that he would take the money after all. "Let the Christian go," he muttered.

"Tarry, Jew. The law hath yet another hold on you," said the lawyer, explaining that as Shylock had sought to kill a citizen of Venice, the punishment was death, should the duke decree it.

"That thou shalt see the difference of our spirits, I pardon thee thy life before thou ask for it," announced the duke.

The duke went on to tell Shylock that half his wealth must go to Antonio and the other half to the state. But Antonio didn't want Shylock's money. Instead he asked that his half of Shylock's estate be given to Shylock's daughter, Jessica. So it was agreed, and Shylock left the court humiliated and muttering oaths against all the world.

The lawyer had saved Antonio's life! Bassanio was overwhelmed with relief. He tried to give the lawyer the three thousand ducats that Antonio had owed Shylock, but the lawyer would not take a fee. Instead he asked for Bassanio's ring. Bassanio refused, for it was the ring that Portia had given him.

"My lord Bassanio, let him have the ring," begged Antonio, for to him a ring seemed a paltry reward for the lawyer who had saved his life.

"Go, Gratiano; run and overtake him; give him the ring," sighed Bassanio, taking it off his finger.

Gratiano went after the lawyer with the ring, which he gratefully accepted. The lawyer's clerk then persuaded Gratiano to part with his ring too. Both he and Bassanio looked down at their naked fingers and wondered what they would tell their wives.

Bassanio, Gratiano and Antonio did not tarry in Venice, but returned to Belmont as quickly as the journey allowed. When they reached Portia's home, they never guessed that Portia and Nerissa had only returned a few moments before them.

"You are welcome home, my lord," cried Portia.

"Give welcome to my friend: this is the man, this is Antonio," said Bassiano.

At first the wives seemed pleased to see their husbands. Then Nerissa looked at Gratiano's hands and asked where the ring was that she had given him. "You swore to me, when I did give it you, that you would wear it till your hour of death!" she shouted.

"A quarrel, ho, already! What's the matter?" asked Portia.

Soon both Gratiano and Bassanio were in trouble over their lost rings!

"Sweet Portia, if you did know to whom I gave the ring," pleaded Bassanio.

Both wives were unrelenting and claimed to be deeply upset and offended.

"I am the unhappy subject of these quarrels," said Antonio. He begged the wives to forgive their husbands.

Finally, Portia relented. She bade Antonio pass Bassanio a ring. "And bid him keep it better than the other," she said.

"By heaven! It is the same I gave the doctor!" cried Bassanio.

Then Nerissa relented as well and gave Gratiano a ring. This ring also seemed very familiar. The two men stared at the rings and then at each other. Surely these were the very rings that they had given away?

"Were you the doctor and I knew you not?" asked Bassanio, turning to his wife in amazement.

"Were you the clerk?" asked Gratiano, looking at Nerissa in disbelief.

It was true. Portia had been the young lawyer who had saved Antonio's life, and Nerissa her clerk! The two men could not believe how blind they had been.

There was more good news to come: Nerissa told Jessica that even though she had eloped with Lorenzo, she would inherit Shylock's wealth. And Antonio discovered that his ships had finally come safely into harbour. At last the friends could celebrate and laugh at the husbands who had not known their own wives!

"Well," chuckled Gratiano, swinging his wife high into the air, "while I live, I'll fear no other thing so sore as keeping safe Nerissa's ring."

Julius Caesar

It was a day of celebration and the streets of ancient Rome swarmed with excited citizens – cobblers, carpenters and tradespeople of every kind. They were all dressed in their finest clothes waiting to cheer their hero, Julius Caesar, after a great victory over his rival, Pompey. They brought flowers to garland his statues, and petals and sweet-smelling herbs to throw in his path.

Two tribunes, Flavius and Marullus, tried in vain to clear a way through the streets and control the growing crowd's enthusiasm. "Hence! Home, you idle creatures, get you home," shouted Flavius. "Is this a holiday?"

The citizens' excitement angered Flavius and Marullus, for it wasn't so long ago that these people had cheered Pompey. At this time, Rome was a republic – ruled by the people through their senators. In the past, Romans had fought to rid Rome of the rule of bad and all-powerful monarchs. But now some politicians feared Caesar wished to become king. However, the common people loved him for he was a persuasive orator, and great crowds always gathered to hear him speak.

"We make a holiday to see Caesar, and to rejoice in his triumph!" they cried, undaunted by the tribunes' rising anger.

"You blocks, you stones, you worse than senseless things!" shouted Flavius and Marullus, waving their swords at the crowd.

All their efforts were in vain, for as the drums rolled and the trumpets sounded, Caesar appeared! A great cheer rose from the throng, making even the still waters of the River Tiber tremble. Dressed in purple and wearing the victor's laurel wreath,

Caesar nodded and waved to the adoring crowd. Behind him walked the other greats of Rome, including two senators, Brutus and Cassius, and Caesar's friend Mark Antony who was stripped and ready for the games. For it was the Feast of Lupercal, when noblemen ran naked through the streets.

Suddenly the cheers and trumpets were silenced by a single shrill call for Caesar.

"Ha, who calls?" demanded Caesar.

An ancient soothsayer came out of the crowd and stood, bent and ragged, before the great general. The crowd was hushed by his daring.

"Beware the Ides of March," he said, in a voice that echoed through the streets.

"He is a dreamer," scoffed Caesar. "Let us leave him."

The party moved off to watch the games, but many wondered what the soothsayer meant – the Ides of March were the fifteenth day of the month, which was not far off.

Brutus and Cassius hung back, for they were not in the mood for games – they supported the republic and were sickened by Caesar's triumphant behaviour. They could hear the roar of the crowd as he took his seat for the games.

"What means this shouting?" sighed Brutus. "I do fear the people choose Caesar for their king."

"Ay, do you fear it?" replied Cassius. "Then must I think you would not have it so."

"I would not, Cassius," replied Brutus, reluctantly. For though Brutus loved Caesar, he loved and honoured Rome more, and had no wish to see the return of a monarchy.

Later, the two men heard Caesar and his followers make their way back from the games. Plainly things had not gone well for Caesar – he was looking grim. They called their friend, Casca, to one side.

"Would you speak with me?" Casca asked, nervously.

"Tell us what hath chanc'd today, that Caesar looks so sad," said Brutus.

Casca looked about him, for these were dangerous times and he could not risk being caught making fun of Caesar.

HURRAH! HURRAH! HURRAH!

However, once he saw that they were alone, Casca could hardly contain his laughter as he recounted how Mark Antony had offered Caesar the crown. Caesar had refused it, hoping the crowd would insist he accepted, but instead the crowd had roared its approval! Three times Mark Antony held up the crown and three times the crowd roared and cheered when Caesar refused it.

There was now no doubt in Brutus and Cassius's minds that Caesar wished to be king. Today they had been saved by the citizens, but who would save the republic tomorrow? Even noble Brutus began to consider what might be done, while Cassius's fingers twitched over his dagger.

That night there was a violent storm; it was as though the noise of some great battle hurtled through the skies. On the ground there were strange omens: horses screamed, dying men cried out and ghosts rose from their graves and walked wailing through the streets. It seemed the gods on Mount Olympus knew that Cassius, fearful that the Senate would offer Caesar the crown, conspired to murder Caesar. He had already persuaded Decius, Cinna, Mettellus Cimber and Trebonius to join him, and now he pulled Casca aside.

"Casca, I have mov'd already some certain of the noblest-minded Romans to undergo with me an enterprise," he whispered to his friend.

"O Cassius! If you could but win the noble Brutus to our party," Casca said.

Cassius knew Casca was right. All Rome knew Brutus to be an honourable man, and his name would lend respect to the deed. So Cassius, Casca and the other conspirators secretly made their way to Brutus's house.

Although they made a strong case against Caesar, Brutus was unwilling to join the plot. He wanted what was best for Rome, but it was a terrible thing to murder a friend. "Since Cassius first did whet me against Caesar," he said, "I have not slept." As the sky roared angrily above them, the conspirators laid their plan before

Brutus and finally convinced him. "Give me your hands all over, one by one," he said.

The assassination was planned for the following day, which happened to be the Ides of March. They resolved to kill Caesar in the Senate, before he could accept the crown. "Let's kill him boldly, but not wrathfully," said Brutus, who sought to find some honour in the deed.

In another part of Rome, Caesar's wife, Calpurnia, was dreaming of his death. Three times she cried out in her sleep, "Help, ho! They murder Caesar." When morning came, she begged Caesar to stay home and not go to the Senate. She told him she had had visions of his murder and had seen blood gush from his statues.

"Caesar shall go forth," he snapped. For who, he thought, would dare to harm the great Caesar?

"Alas, my lord, your wisdom is consum'd in confidence," cried Calpurnia, falling to her knees. "You shall not stir out of your house today."

But Caesar was tempted by the rumour that the Senate planned to offer him the crown. "How foolish do your fears seem. Give me my robe, for I will go!"

There was a knock at the door and the senators Publius, Brutus, Ligarius, Metellus, Casca, Trebonius, Cinna and Mark Antony entered, ready to escort Caesar to the Senate. Through the streets they paraded, with Caesar in high spirits. He nodded and waved most regally to the early morning crowds, certain that by the evening he would wear the crown. Even when he met the soothsayer on the Senate steps, he was not upset.

"The Ides of March are come," he laughed.

"Aye Caesar; but not gone," came the chilling reply.

Inside the Senate, while Caesar listened to a petition, the conspirators slowly gathered round him, Cassius behind him and the others in front. Suddenly, without any warning, they all drew their daggers. Each one stabbed Caesar in turn. The last to stab Caesar was Brutus.

"Et tu, Brute?" cried Caesar. "Then fall, Caesar!"

"Liberty! Freedom! Tyranny is dead!" yelled Cinna. "Run hence, proclaim, cry it about the streets!"

As Caesar fell dead upon the floor, the other senators fled in fear and confusion.

"Fly not, stand still," shouted Brutus. "Ambition's debt is paid."

But they were gone. Only Mark Antony returned to grieve for his friend.

"Welcome, Mark Antony," said Brutus.

"O mighty Caesar! Dost thou lie so low?" cried Antony, falling to his knees beside Caesar's body. He turned to the conspirators and begged them to kill him too, if they bore him any grudge, but Brutus wanted no more bloodshed. He promised Antony that their reasons for killing Caesar were justified. "We will deliver you the cause why I, that did love Caesar when I struck him, have thus proceeded," he said.

Mark Antony asked if he could speak at Caesar's funeral as his friend and admirer, and against Cassius's advice, Brutus agreed.

"You know not what you do," said Cassius. "Do not consent." But it was too late.

Left alone with Caesar's lifeless body, Antony looked upon the bloody, open wounds and swore that he would avenge his friend's violent death. "Thou art the ruins of the noblest man that ever lived in the tide of times," he said, holding Caesar's body in his arms. "Woe to the hand that shed this costly blood!"

News of Caesar's death spread like wildfire through the city. By the time Brutus left the Senate, an angry throng had gathered. Their hero had been killed and now they wanted revenge. Brutus raised his hands for silence and the crowd was hushed.

"Romans, countrymen and lovers," he said. "As Caesar loved me, I weep for him, as he was valiant, I honour him: but, as he was ambitious, I slew him."

Brutus, with fine words and much passion, explained to Rome's shocked citizens that Caesar had threatened their freedom. He called for them to speak against him if they believed he had done wrong, but none did. A great cheer went up for Brutus, and if he had not insisted that every citizen should stay to hear Mark Antony, he would have been carried home as their hero. As Brutus departed, Caesar's body was brought forth and laid upon a bier. Mark Antony began to speak. At first nobody would listen to him, but gradually the emotion in his voice silenced the crowd.

"Friends, Romans, countrymen, lend me your ears," he began. "I come to bury Caesar, not to praise him. The evil that men do lives after them; the good is oft interred with their bones."

Antony spoke of Caesar's great love for the people and told the crowd he had left money to each of them, and his gardens and orchards to all. Then Antony lifted up Caesar's mantle and showed the rapt citizens the dagger marks. Everyone that watched Antony could feel the wounds themselves, so impassioned was his speech.

"O piteous spectacle!" cried one citizen.

"O noble Caesar!" cried another.

Mark Antony had succeeded – he had turned the crowd against the conspirators. Holding Caesar's body aloft like a trophy, the people swept through the streets, searching for his murderers, burning and looting as they went. With the citizens behind him, Antony knew he could drive out his enemies. "Now let it work: mischief, thou art afoot," he whispered to himself. "Take thou what course thou wilt!"

Pursued by the angry mob, the conspirators were forced to flee the city, but they were determined to return. Over the following months, Brutus and Cassius both raised armies, intending to retake Rome.

Meanwhile, Mark Antony formed an alliance with Octavius, Caesar's lawful heir. They too began to raise an army. To pay for their legions, they stole the money Caesar had left the citizens of Rome.

In raising money for their armies, Brutus and Cassius quarrelled violently. Cassius had refused Brutus money for his army and had also defended a soldier who had taken bribes. Brutus's nobility was offended by these acts.

"Go to; you are not Cassius," he shouted.

"I am," replied his friend. "You love me not."

"I do not like your faults," Brutus declared.

"There is my dagger," said Cassius.

But Brutus had had enough. "Sheathe your dagger," he cried. "I am sick of many griefs." He confessed that his ill humour was caused by overwhelming sadness. His

beloved wife, Portia, unable to bear being separated from him, had killed herself.

"O insupportable and touching loss!" cried Cassius, forgetting his anger and hugging his friend.

As Cassius comforted Brutus, news arrived that Mark Antony and Octavius were marching to Philippi with a powerful army. This was not what Cassius and Brutus had expected. They decided that they would join forces with the remaining conspirators and set out for Philippi to confront their enemy, which was most unwise and just what Antony hoped for. He knew that the march was long and hard and would exhaust the conspirators' legions before the fighting even began.

The night before the battle, while the conspirators and their army were camped outside Philippi, Brutus held out his hands to Cassius. "If we do meet again, why, we shall smile," he said. "If not, why then this parting is well made."

"For ever and for ever, farewell, Brutus!" replied Cassius.

When the first pink rays of dawn broke, the drums rolled and the battle for Rome began. All day it raged: swords clashed and men and horses screamed. First it seemed

one side was winning and then the other. However, as the day wore on, it was clear that Brutus and Cassius's armies, weakened by the long march to Philippi, were no match for the enemy – and as the sun set on their swords, they had to admit their defeat.

Cassius fell upon his own sword rather than witness the fall of the Roman republic, along with many others who had not died in battle. Many more fled – but as darkness fell and the eerie sound of the wounded and dying replaced the noise of battle, Brutus was still on the field. He lit a torch and held it aloft, searching amongst the wounded. Surely there must be one soldier left with the strength to hold his sword steady whilst he fell upon it? Brutus was weary and felt his bones were ready to rest.

Only one soldier stood ready to obey Brutus's last command.

"Hold then my sword, and turn away thy face while I do run upon it," Brutus ordered. "Caesar, now be still: I kill'd not thee with half so good a will."

So Brutus died swiftly and bravely. When Octavius and Antony heard that he was dead, Octavius was eager to celebrate their victory – but Antony paused. First he wanted to pay his respects to Brutus, whom he knew had been motivated to kill Caesar by neither greed nor envy, but by his love for Rome and its people.

This was the noblest Roman of them all. All the conspirators, save only he, did that they did in envy of great Caesar. This was a man!

Much Ado About Nothing

There was such a bustle of excitement at the governor's house in Messina, Sicily. The governor, Leonato, had just received word that guests were about to arrive – and not just any guests! Don Pedro, the Prince of Aragon, was coming with his brother Don John and two handsome young officers – Claudio, a lord of Florence, and Benedick, a lord of Padua. The last time they had visited, they were about to go to war. Now they were returning after a successful campaign and would have time for fun. All the gentlemen arrived dressed to please the ladies – all, that is, except for Seignior Benedick. He was a soldier through and through, so he wore his uniform and his face remained unshaven. Besides, he had no time for ladies and had sworn never to marry.

Leonato had a very sweet daughter called Hero and a beautiful niece called Beatrice. Hero was as charming and good tempered as a summer's day and Beatrice was as sparky and vivid as an autumn storm! Since the gentlemen's last visit, Hero had secretly held a spot in her heart for Seignior Claudio, but Beatrice had no time for men. She found Seignior Benedick particularly annoying and had swapped sharp words with him on every previous visit. It seemed that this occasion was to be no different.

"What! My dear Lady Disdain, Are you yet living?" said Benedick. "Is it possible Disdain should die, while she hath such meet food to feed it as Seignior Benedick?" countered Beatrice.

The greeting between Hero and Claudio went very differently, for although not a word passed between them, Claudio could not take his eyes off the lady. He felt himself being captured by her gentle innocence and he could hardly wait to discuss the matter with Benedick.

"Benedick, didst thou note the daughter of Seignior Leonato?" he burst out. "In mine eye she is the sweetest lady that I ever looked on."

"I can see yet without spectacles and I see no such matter," replied his friend.

Don Pedro, on the other hand, was a true romantic and was delighted to hear that Claudio had fallen in love with such a suitable young lady. He promised to further Claudio's suit at the masked ball to be held that very evening.

Then Don Pedro turned to Benedick, who was noisily declaring he would live and die a bachelor. "I shall see thee, ere I die, look pale with love," promised Don Pedro.

"With anger, with sickness, or with hunger, my lord, not with love!" Benedick assured him.

Later that night, amidst the merry music and dancing, Benedick and Beatrice continued their sparring. Hero, on the other hand, had only soft words to speak to her Claudio, and before the evening ended Don Pedro had gained her father's consent to a marriage. Claudio was speechless with gratitude and delight!

"Speak, count, 'tis your cue," laughed Beatrice.

"Silence is the perfectest herald of joy," cried Claudio, eventually finding his voice. "I were but a little happy, if I could say how much."

"Good Lord, for alliance! Thus goes everyone to the world but I," said Beatrice, with an unconvincing sigh. "I may sit in the corner and cry heigh-ho for a husband!"

With that, the lady vanished into the night, leaving Don Pedro wondering, just wondering, if having managed one love match, he might not arrange another …

"She were an excellent wife for Benedick," he announced, delighted with the thought.

"Oh Lord!" exclaimed Leonato in horror. "My lord, if they were but a week married, they would talk themselves mad!"

However, Don Pedro was not to be dissuaded. "I will bring Seignior Benedick and the lady Beatrice into a mountain of affection the one with the other," he promised. Claudio, Hero and Leonato agreed to help him, even though they thought it a mad idea with not a chance of success. For no two people were more eager to stay single than Beatrice and Benedick.

The following day, the three conspirators set about their task. As Benedick was resting alone in the arbour in Leonato's garden, Don Pedro, Claudio

and Leonato passed close by. Benedick just happened to overhear them say that Beatrice was sick with love for him.

"What was it you told me of today, that your niece Beatrice was in love with Seignior Benedick?" said Don Pedro casually, if a touch too loudly.

"She loves him with an enraged affection," declared the count.

"Tears her hair, prays, curses, O sweet Benedick!" said Claudio.

Benedick was most amazed. To begin with he thought it must be some trick, but then he felt convinced that Leonato would not lie. "This can be no trick," he thought. "Love me! It must be requited! When I said I would die a bachelor, I did not think I should live till I was married," he informed the bees that buzzed around the arbour.

So the conspirators had hooked their first fish! Benedick had believed them. He resolved to give up being proud and love Beatrice back.

Later that same morning, Beatrice was resting alone in the arbour in Leonato's garden, when Hero and her maid Ursula passed close by. Beatrice just happened to overhear them say that Benedick was sick with love for her.

"But are you sure that Benedick loves Beatrice so entirely?" Ursula quizzed her mistress.

"So says the prince and my new-trothed lord," declared Hero, in her most innocent voice.

Beatrice was amazed – almost more amazed than Benedick had been to hear that she loved him. "What fire is in mine ears?" she wondered. "Can this be true?" Yet Beatrice felt convinced that her sweet cousin would not lie. She would have to believe her friends. In an instant, she resolved to give up being haughty and return Benedick's love. "Contempt, farewell! And, Benedick, love on; I will requite thee," she cried.

Meanwhile, Don Pedro's spiteful brother Don John and his cohort Borachio were plotting to ruin Hero's wedding plans. Don John hated his brother and would do anything to upset him. So when he heard that Don Pedro had arranged the wedding of Claudio and Hero for the following day, he vowed to destroy the happy event.

"It is so; the count Claudio shall marry the daughter of Leonato?" he asked Borachio.

"Yea, my lord; but I can cross it," Borachio replied with a sneer.

Don John smiled at the thought. He handed Borachio a large sum of money. Then he listened eagerly to Borachio's plan and shook Borachio warmly by the hand.

Later that night, Don John persuaded Don Pedro and Claudio to stand under one of the upstairs windows of Leonato's house. Standing hidden in the shadows, they looked up and saw they were below Hero's bedroom – and then they thought they saw Hero embrace Borachio and whisper in his

ear. Claudio could not believe his eyes: surely his sweet Hero would not behave in such a terrible, disloyal way? Yet he could not deny the evidence of his own eyes.

At first he was numb with shock, but then he felt foolish for believing her sweet, innocent looks and he was overcome with anger and hatred for her. He decided to show the whole household what a deceiving minx Hero was.

The following day, an excited party gathered inside the local church to celebrate the wedding of Claudio and Hero. Hero smiled happily as she joined Claudio at the altar – but just as Friar Francis was about to marry them, Claudio turned on Hero and accused her of disloyalty.

A gasp ran round the chapel. How could this be? Leonato's lovely daughter? Yet Claudio was not to be checked.

"Give not this rotten orange to your friend," he shouted at Leonato. "She's but a sign and semblance of her honour."

"Is my lord well, that he doth speak so wide?" cried Hero.

"What do you mean, my lord?" cried Leonato, astonished and hurt that his daughter should be slandered in this way. However, when Don Pedro also bore witness against Hero, even her own father began to believe the terrible accusation. Overcome by shock and heartache, Hero fell to the ground in a deathlike trance.

"How doth the lady?" asked Benedick.

"Dead I think! Help, Uncle! Hero, Uncle, Seignior Benedick, Friar!" cried Beatrice in rising panic.

As the wedding guests left the church, Hero's colour gradually returned and her eyes opened. The friar, who knew Hero would never have committed such a sin, thought her faint might be used to advantage. "Let her awhile be secretly kept in," he said, "and publish it that she is dead indeed." He hoped that the false news of her death might knock some sense into Claudio.

Meanwhile, shocked and upset that her cousin had been slandered in such a manner, Beatrice could not stop her tears. When Benedick saw this, he was overcome with pity for her. Suddenly he could control himself no longer and he blurted out his love for her.

"I do love nothing in the world so well as you: is not that strange," he said, waiting to be rebuffed.

"I love you with so much of my heart that none is left to protest," came the unexpected answer.

On a cloud of happiness, Benedick asked Beatrice to bid him do anything to prove his love and to stem her tears, but he was horrified by Beatrice's chill request:

"Kill Claudio."

"Ha! Not for the wide world," cried Benedick.

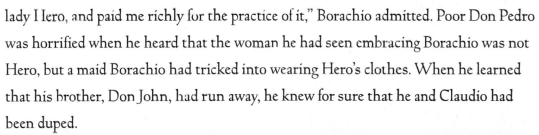

"You kill me to deny it," said Beatrice. "Farewell."

Benedick could not bear to lose Beatrice's love so soon after winning it, so after much persuasion he agreed to fight his friend.

Luckily for Benedick, before the fight could take place, Borachio was heard by the night watch talking about his conspiracy with Don John. "Therefore know, I have earned of Don John a thousand ducats," Borachio boasted.

Borachio was arrested and forced to confess to Don Pedro. "Don John your brother incensed me to slander the lady Hero, and paid me richly for the practice of it," Borachio admitted. Poor Don Pedro was horrified when he heard that the woman he had seen embracing Borachio was not Hero, but a maid Borachio had tricked into wearing Hero's clothes. When he learned that his brother, Don John, had run away, he knew for sure that he and Claudio had been duped.

Claudio was filled with remorse for having, as he believed, caused sweet Hero's death. "Impose me to what penance your invention can lay upon my sin," he begged.

"I cannot bid you bid my daughter live," said Leonato, feigning a broken heart.

Leonato instructed Claudio instead to spend the night beside Hero's tomb, singing of her innocence, and to go back to the church the following morning and marry Hero's cousin, whom he did not know. Claudio was so filled with shame that he was prepared to agree to anything. So that night he made his way to a tomb prepared for Hero and spent the night in tears and song.

As morning broke and the wedding bells rang out, Claudio made his way to church. His heart was heavy, but he was determined to take his punishment and marry Hero's cousin, even if she was as ugly and bristly as a broom. Two ladies arrived and walked down the aisle towards him, hidden behind masks.

"Are you yet determin'd today to marry with my brother's daughter?" asked Leonato.

"I'll hold my mind." replied Claudio. "Which is the lady I must seize upon?"

"This same is she, and I do give you to her," replied Leonato's brother, Antonio.

The first lady removed her mask – but she was not Hero's unknown cousin. She was Hero herself! Claudio was overcome with amazement. "Another Hero!" he cried.

"Nothing certainer," smiled Hero. "One Hero died defil'd, but I do live!"

"The former Hero!" exclaimed Don Pedro in delight. "Hero that is dead!"

"She died, my lord, but whiles her slander liv'd," answered Leonato.

Then everyone turned as the second lady removed her mask. There stood Beatrice, looking every inch the modest bride, but still bent on teasing her beloved Benedick.

"Do not you love me?" asked Benedick hopefully.

"Why, no," she replied, "no more than reason."

"Come, Cousin," laughed Leonato, "I am sure you love the gentleman."

"And I'll be sworn upon't that he loves her," declared Claudio.

After much playful banter between Beatrice and Benedick which Benedick finally managed to put a stop to with a kiss, Beatrice and Benedick agreed to wed.

Friar Francis and all the reassembled guests cheered with delight, for all believed that the couples were perfectly matched. Without further ado, Friar Francis united them in matrimony. Even Beatrice and Benedick, who had so scorned marriage, seemed overcome with joy.

When news arrived that Don John had been captured, the wedding party decided to think of a punishment for him another time. They revelled in their happiness, and feasted and danced through the sun-filled day and the sweet-scented Sicilian night!

King Lear

In ancient Britain, the elderly King Lear was feeling tired. The burdens of state had worn him down and in his old age he just wanted to enjoy being king. So Lear decided to divide his kingdom among his three daughters, keeping only the crown for himself. Excited by the prospect of giving up his lands and power and being able to relax, he summoned his daughters to his palace along with all his knights and nobles. There, on a fond father's whim, he declared that he would give the largest territory to the daughter who professed to love him best.

The gathered lords and nobles frowned at this division of the kingdom, particularly the Earl of Kent, Lear's loyal friend. However, the old king was in no doubt that his favourite and youngest daughter, Cordelia, would profess the deepest love. So he sat on his throne, happily waiting to bask in his daughters' declarations of adoration.

His eldest daughter, greedy Goneril of Albany, was the first to respond. She cared not one jot for her father, but she cared for power and wealth, so she pretended to love her father very much indeed.

"Sir," she cried on bended knee, "I do love you more than words can wield the matter; dearer than eyesight, space, and liberty." When Goneril was finished, King Lear clapped his old hands in delight and gave her one third of his kingdom.

Then came Lear's second daughter, Regan of Cornwall, with white, wafer-thin lips. Regan's love was as shallow as her greed was deep, but she swore she loved her father even more than

Goneril did. "I am made of that self mettle as my sister," she said. "Only she comes too short." For her false words, Lear gave Regan a portion of his kingdom to match Goneril's.

Then Lear turned to his youngest, Cordelia. "Now, our joy," he said proudly. "What can you say to draw a third more opulent than your sisters? Speak."

"Nothing, my lord," replied Cordelia.

"Nothing?" exclaimed the king, hardly able to believe his ears.

"Nothing," said Cordelia.

"Nothing will come of nothing. Speak again," shouted the king.

Poor Cordelia was unable to put her thoughts into words – she loved her father so much and so truly. She had been sickened by her sisters' false words, and she could not bring herself to compete with their falsehood. All her young life, Cordelia had shown her father both love and respect. Surely she had nothing to prove?

"I love Your Majesty according to my bond," said Cordelia. "Nor more nor less."

"So young, and so untender?" cried her father.

"So young, my lord, and true," replied Cordelia.

At this, Lear flew into a rage. He felt that Cordelia had made a fool of him in front of his whole court. He disowned Cordelia and divided the best lands that he had saved for her between Goneril and Regan.

"Check this hideous rashness," cried the Earl of Kent. Kent could not believe that Lear had trusted his two stone-hearted daughters and not understood his youngest daughter's true and loving heart. But Lear was in no mood to listen to anyone. He banished Kent on the spot. "Away! If thy banish'd trunk be found in our dominions, the moment is thy death!" the king roared.

Kent was not the only noble to admire and understand Cordelia's honesty. Her suitor, the King of France, was moved by her brave conduct. Far from deserting her now that she was without an inheritance, he asked her to marry him.

"Fairest Cordelia, that art most rich, being poor. Thee and thy virtues here I seize upon," he said.

"Thou hast her, France," snarled Lear, "let her be thine, for we have no such daughter."

So Cordelia prepared to sail for France, reluctantly leaving her father in the care of her cunning sisters.

The banished Kent could see troubled times ahead for Lear and could not bring himself to leave his old friend. He disguised himself as a commoner and took a job as Lear's servant, hoping to protect him from his scheming daughters.

Lear had no palace of his own now, so he took one hundred knights, his fool and his new servant to stay with Goneril, in a castle that just hours before had been his.

Goneril and her husband, the Duke of Albany, made no pretence of welcoming the old king. Goneril was no longer the daughter full of loving promises, for she already had everything her father had to give – she had even taken his crown. As the days went by, Goneril treated the old king without any love or respect. Soon even Goneril's servants refused to do the king's bidding.

"How now, Daughter?" said Lear. "Methinks you are too much of late i' th' frown."

"I lere do you keep a hundred knights and squires," she snapped back at him. "Men so disordered, so debauched and bold that this our court, infected with their manners, shows like a riotous inn."

This was quite untrue, for the king's knights and squires were noble men who had been with him for many years. King Lear was stung by his daughter's ingratitude, and tears came to his eyes.

"How sharper than a serpent's tooth it is to have a thankless child!" he cried. "I have another daughter, who, I am sure, is kind and comfortable."

Bewildered by Goneril's harshness, Lear decided to visit Regan, who he felt sure would be kinder. He sent his new servant ahead to the Earl of Gloucester's palace, where Regan and her husband, the Duke of Cornwall, were staying. Then he, his knights and his loyal fool followed, galloping wildly through the night.

They arrived at Gloucester's palace as dawn broke – but there was no welcome for them there. All that greeted them was Lear's servant in the stocks. Lear was outraged that a servant of his had been treated with such disrespect. "They durst not do't; They could not, would not do't," muttered the king, fearing that he might be going mad.

He sent for Regan to come and explain herself. She came out with Goneril by her side. Lear realized that Goneril had ridden ahead and that his two daughters had joined forces against him. They told Lear he must give up his knights and live as a pauper.

"What need you five-and-twenty, ten, or five?" snapped Goneril.

"What need one?" said Regan through her thin white lips.

"I gave you all!" the king cried out. He had no other daughter left to turn to. How bitterly he regretted casting off Cordelia.

King Lear rushed out onto the heath in a pitiless storm, his mind twisting in pain and sorrow. The lashing rain was nothing compared with the lashing tongues of his daughters. Lear's fool, and his faithful companion, Kent, ran after him.

"O Fool! I shall go mad!" Lear shouted through the wind. "Blow, winds, and crack your cheeks! Rage! Blow!"

The Earl of Gloucester, powerless against Goneril and Regan, sadly watched Lear stumble across the heath. He too had suffered at the hands of his children. His youngest son, Edmund, had told him that Edgar, his favourite son, planned to murder him. This was a lie, but Gloucester had believed it and had driven Edgar away. He did not know that Edgar was living nearby in a hovel on the heath, disguised as a mad beggar. It was into this very hovel that Kent and the fool dragged King Lear for shelter.

"He that has a little tiny wit,

With hey, ho, the wind and the rain,

Must make content with his fortunes fit,

Though the rain it raineth every day," sang the fool,

brushing the rain off the king.

Edgar cowered in the shadows, naked but for a rag around his waist, delirious with cold and misery. "Pillicock sat on Pillicock Hill," he cried. "Halloo, halloo, loo, loo!"

"This cold night will turn us all to fools and madmen," shivered the fool.

"Tom's a-cold," moaned Edgar.

The old king looked at this bundle of jabbering rags with pity. "Didst thou give all to thy two daughters?" he asked. "And art thou come to this?"

The wind and the rain continued to howl outside while King Lear and his motley companions tried to shut their eyes to the night and the biting cold.

Back at the palace, Gloucester overheard Regan and Goneril plotting to kill King Lear. Bravely he rushed out into the night to warn Kent.

"Come hither, friend: where is the king, my master?" he said.

"Here, sir; but trouble him not. His wits are gone," Kent replied.

"I have o'erheard a plot of death upon him. There is a litter ready; lay him in it and drive towards Dover," said brave Gloucester. So Kent and the fool carried King Lear towards the coast.

On his return to the castle, Gloucester discovered that he had been seen helping the

old king. On the orders of Goneril and Regan, he was dragged across the great hall of the castle and bound fast to a chair.

"I shall see the winged vengeance overtake such children," he cried bravely.

"See't shalt thou never," cried Cornwall, and brutally tore out one of his eyes.

A shocked servant tried to intervene. He was swiftly killed, but not before he had wounded Cornwall. Oblivious to his wound and urged on by Regan, Cornwall took out Gloucester's other eye. "Out, vile jelly!" he cried.

When Regan heard that Cornwall's wound had proved fatal, she was delighted. Now her husband was dead, she was free to marry Gloucester's scheming son, Edmund, whom she loved. Unfortunately, Goneril loved him too, and was consumed with jealousy. She wrote to Edmund suggesting he kill her husband, Albany, leaving her free to marry him.

But the sisters had to put their battle for Edmund to one side: news came that Cordelia, having heard of her father's plight, had raised a French army and landed at Dover. The two sisters marshalled their troops and set off to fight Cordelia.

Kent had also heard that Cordelia had landed. He took Lear to look for her, hoping to reunite father and daughter. Blind Gloucester was on his way to Dover, too, with his son Edgar, who had found him lost on the heath. Outside the port, Gloucester, now eyeless, met Lear, mad with misery and fatigue. The king was almost naked and on his head he wore a lopsided crown made of flowers and herbs. "I am the king himself," he said. But none would have known it.

As the war drums rolled, Cordelia's servants came searching for the king. "O! Here he is; lay hand upon him," ordered the captain.

Poor Lear was more confused than ever when he was carried to the French camp.

The surgeons would not let him see Cordelia until he had rested, as they feared that the shock of seeing her again might kill him.

When at last Lear woke and found Cordelia kneeling beside him, he could not believe his sad old eyes. "Do not laugh at me; for, as I am a man, I think this lady to be my child Cordelia," he said to Kent and the doctor.

"And so I am, I am," wept Cordelia, hardly able to bear the sight of what her cruel sisters had done to her father.

As Lear drifted in and out of sleep, Cordelia reluctantly left him, for the drums of war were still beating. King Lear slept through the long and hard-fought battle. When he awoke, Cordelia and the French had been defeated. Cordelia could have escaped, but she chose to stay with her father. Lear rejoiced, for the idea of imprisonment with Cordelia was heaven compared with liberty with Goneril and Regan. He refused to try and bargain with them for his freedom. "No, no, no, no!" he cried to Cordelia. "Come, let's away to prison. We two alone will sing like birds i' the cage."

As Lear and Cordelia were led away, Edmund called the captain to him. He gave orders that they both should be killed.

Shortly after the captain left to carry out this heartless deed, Albany arrived with Goneril and Regan. He had discovered Goneril and Edmund's plan to kill him! "Edmund, I arrest thee on capital treason, and this gilded serpent," he snarled, pointing to his wife.

But before the guards could lay hold of Edmund, an armoured man stepped from the crowd and challenged Edmund to a duel. "Draw thy sword," cried the stranger.

Edmund accepted the challenge and the duel began. Goneril and Regan watched in horror as Edmund began to lose to his unknown opponent. After the stranger had delivered a mortal blow to Edmund, he removed his helmet and revealed himself. "My name is Edgar, and thy father's son," he said.

"The wheel is come full circle," sighed Edmund.

As Edmund lay dying, Edgar told him how he had been reunited with their father, Gloucester, just before his death.

A servant brought news that Goneril had poisoned Regan and then, realizing Edmund would not live, had killed herself too. Edmund was conscience-stricken at last, for he had promised to marry both sisters. With his final breath he told Edgar to send a reprieve for Lear and Cordelia. "Nay, send in time," he cried.

"Run, run! O run!" cried out Albany, appalled at the thought of more bloodshed.

It was too late. Lear's dearest Cordelia had been hanged. Albany and Edgar watched in horror as the old king stumbled towards them carrying her body in his arms.

"Howl, howl, howl, howl!" he wept. "O! You are men of stones: had I your tongues and eyes, I'd use them so that heaven's vaults should crack. She's gone forever."

Beside himself with grief, Lear fell into a faint. He had lost everything – what he had not given away had been taken from him. Even his fool had been executed.

Kent, who the king still did not recognize, knew Lear would never find peace in this world. He watched with relief as his friend's life gently ebbed away, his arms around his only true daughter, Cordelia.

Albany tried to persuade Kent to take the crown, but the old earl had no use for life without Lear. "I have a journey, sir, shortly to go," said Kent. "My master calls me. I must not say no."

So Edgar became king, and tried to rule with honour in memory of two wronged men: his father, the Earl of Gloucester, and King Lear.

The Winter's Tale

King Leontes of Sicily was feeling grumpy – there was too much bustle at court. His beloved wife, Queen Hermione, was expecting their second child any day now, so all her ladies were rushing around in high excitement; their young son, Prince Mamillius, was entertaining everyone with his most exciting tales; and Leontes' good friend, King Polixenes, was preparing to return to his own kingdom of Bohemia.

Polixenes was Leontes' oldest and dearest friend, and he had been staying with Leontes for the past nine months. It had been a grand time and the two men had delighted in sharing childhood memories, but now Polixenes was eager to depart. The winter weather was closing in and he was missing his own son, Prince Florizel.

Polixenes hugged his friend warmly and thanked him for his hospitality.

"Stay your thanks a while; and pay them when you part," replied Leontes, shrugging his friend off.

"Sir, that's tomorrow," smiled Polixenes.

Leontes did not return the smile. He had tried and failed to persuade his old friend to stay. In a final effort to get Polixenes to change his plans, he asked Queen Hermione to persuade Polixenes to delay his departure.

To please her husband, Hermione used all her feminine wiles to cajole Polixenes into staying. Finally she succeeded. "He'll stay, my lord," she cried triumphantly.

"At my request he would not," replied Leontes, feeling a sudden rush of jealousy.

Hermione laughed at her husband's ungracious response and gave Polixenes her hand in gratitude.

Leontes fixed his eyes upon their linked hands and his heart began to thunder against his chest. "My heart dances; but not for joy," he muttered to himself. He stomped off, leaving Hermione to entertain his friend.

"He something seems unsettled," said Hermione, hoping that his mood would pass if he was left to himself.

However, the jealousy that had taken hold of Leontes was not shifted that easily. Faster and louder beat his heart, until it had driven all sane thoughts from his head. His wife had never shown herself to be anything but loving and faithful, and Polixenes was like a brother to him, yet Leontes was now convinced that the pair were in love.

In a state of rage, he went to see Lord Camillo, his friend and advisor. "My wife is slippery," he informed him.

"Good my lord, be cur'd of this diseas'd opinion, for 'tis most dangerous," Camillo cried.

"Say it be, 'tis true," said the king, furious that Camillo dared to argue with him.

"No, no, my lord," said Camillo, who was certain Queen Hermione loved Leontes.

"It is; you lie, you lie," cried Leontes, beside himself with anger and jealousy. "I say thou liest, Camillo, and I hate thee."

Camillo was shocked by Leontes fury – but there was something more shocking to come: Leontes asked him to poison a cup and kill Polixenes. The king grabbed Camillo's jacket and held him close. "Do't, and thou hast the one half of my heart," he promised. "Do't not, thou split'st thine own."

Camillo was left shaken and trembling by this terrible request. Could Leontes be serious? If so, must Camillo obey his king's command and murder an innocent man?

For Camillo did not doubt that King Polixenes was innocent.

"Methinks my favour here begins to warp," thought Camillo uneasily.

Camillo decided to tell Polixenes of Leontes' wicked plan and flee with him to Bohemia that very night. Leontes seemed to have been struck by a terrible disease of the mind, but Camillo was sure he would soon recover. Then he would be able to return to Sicily.

The whole court soon became aware of the king's anger. Hermione was confused and hurt by her husband's sudden coldness and took comfort in her little son, Mamillius. She sat with him in front of a warm fire while he tried to think up an exciting story to distract her.

"A sad tale's best for winter," he said, stroking her hand. "I have one of sprites and goblins."

"Let's have that, good sir," smiled his mother sadly.

"There was a man," said Mamillius, in a ghostly whisper, "dwelt by a churchyard—"

But Mamillius never got any further with his tale, for at that moment his father burst through the door, followed by his armed guards.

"Bear the boy hence; he shall not come about her," Leontes ordered, determined that Hermione should have nothing more to do with the young prince. "Away with her to prison!"

Mamillius cried out for his mother, but Leontes was unmoved. Camillo and Polixenes had escaped earlier that night, and he was now convinced that they and Queen Hermione were plotting to murder him!

Hermione bore all this with quiet dignity, sure that her husband would soon return to his senses. She asked only that she might take her ladies and her friend Paulina to prison with her, for her baby was about to be born.

The rest of the court looked on in horror at these events.

"Be certain what you do, sir, lest your justice prove violence," one lord dared to say.

"Beseech your highness call the queen again," begged another.

But Leontes just grew angrier. "Hold your peaces!" he yelled.

Mamillius was heartbroken to think of his adored mother in jail and refused to eat. Day after day the prince grew weaker, but still Leontes would not repent. He was determined to bring his wife to court and see her sentenced to death. Hoping to silence the many courtiers who doubted his wife's guilt, he sent two lords to consult the Oracle at Delphi in Greece.

Meanwhile, in prison, Hermione gave birth to a daughter, Perdita. Her friend Paulina, in a bid to soften Leontes' heart, wrapped the baby in Hermione's favourite shawl, fixed it with one of her brooches and presented her to Leontes.

"The good queen, for she is good," said brave Paulina, "hath brought you forth a daughter: here 'tis; commends it to your blessing."

"Out!" yelled Leontes furiously. "A mankind witch! Hence with her, out o' door!"

"I pray you, do not push me: I'll be gone," said Paulina. "Look to your babe, my lord; 'tis yours."

Paulina left little Perdita at the king's feet. Leontes looked down on the infant with loathing, convinced that she was not his child but Polixenes'.

"This brat is none of mine. Take it up. I'll not rear another's issue," he yelled at Antigonus, Paulina's husband. He ordered him to take Perdita and set sail for some foreign shore, and there abandon Perdita to her fate.

"Come on, poor babe," crooned Antigonus, as he lifted Perdita into his arms and carried her away from the king's wrath.

Leontes decided he would not wait to hear what the Oracle decreed and he ordered Hermione's trial to start at once. Hermione entered the court with her ladies and her friend Paulina, her head held high. As soon as the court sat and the session began, the two messengers returned from Delphi. After swearing that the Oracle had not been tampered with, one of the lords read out its secrets to the court.

"Hermione is chaste; Polixenes blameless; Camillo a true subject; Leontes a jealous tyrant; his innocent babe truly begotten; and the king shall live without an heir, if that which is lost be not found."

The Oracle had proclaimed Hermione innocent!

"Now blessed be the great Apollo!" cried the whole court – apart from Leontes.

"There is no truth at all i' the Oracle, the sessions shall proceed," he ordered.

Then all of a sudden, a servant ran in to the courtroom. He had terrible news to report: Mamillius, overwhelmed by sorrow, had suddenly died. A gasp of horror went round the court and Hermione collapsed to the floor.

"This news is mortal to the queen," sobbed Paulina, as she helped to carry Hermione from the courtroom.

Suddenly Leontes' madness seemed to leave him and he woke to the terrible harm his wicked jealousy had caused. "Apollo's angry; and the heavens themselves do strike at my injustice," he cried. He fell to his knees and begged Apollo for forgiveness. But his repentance came too late, for Paulina returned to tell him that Hermione had also died. Her poor heart had been unable to take the pain of losing her two children and her husband's love. Paulina railed against Leontes in her misery.

The king was desolate and deeply ashamed, and he took every angry word that Paulina threw at him as his due punishment. He swore to her that he would live a life of mourning.

"Will you swear never to marry but by my free leave?" shouted Paulina.

"Never, Paulina: so be my blessed spirit," he swore.

Meanwhile out at sea, a storm had hit the ship carrying Antigonus and Perdita and driven it onto the shores of Bohemia. The ship and all its crew were lost to the rocks and the raging sea, but Antigonus managed to wade ashore with Perdita safe in his arms, still wrapped in Hermione's shawl. As the rain lashed at his face, he found shelter for this tiny bundle between two rocks. There he left Perdita to her fate. He turned back towards the sea, hoping to find a ship that would take him back to Sicily – but as he slipped and scrambled across the rocks, a huge bear reared up at him out of the darkness. Poor Antigonus was never heard of again.

Luckily, Perdita was found by a shepherd who was out looking for lost sheep. He took her home to his wife, and they cared for her as a daughter for the next fifteen years.

Perdita grew into a beautiful young woman, and although she was brought up as a shepherdess, she had all the natural charm and grace of a princess. Indeed, when Prince Florizel, son of King Polixenes, met her whilst out hunting, he fell in love with her in an instant.

"I bless the time when my good falcon made her flight across thy father's ground," he said to Perdita. For if it hadn't been for the falcon, how would a prince ever have met and fallen in love with a shepherd's daughter?

Lord Camillo, who was living with Florizel and King Polixenes at their palace, would have been astonished if he had known that his old friend King Leontes' daughter was living as a shepherdess just a few miles from the palace.

Camillo longed to return to Sicily – he had heard that Leontes had recovered from his madness and now lived a quiet and gentle life. However, King Polixenes would not hear of Camillo leaving, for he had come to rely on his advice. Indeed, when Polixenes heard rumours that his son was courting a lowly shepherd's daughter, he turned at once to Camillo. He wanted to meet Perdita for himself, and wanted Camillo to go with him.

The two men disguised themselves as peasants and set off for Perdita's home. There they found Florizel and Perdita, and were astonished to be asked to witness their engagement. So complete were their disguises that Florizel hadn't even recognized his own father. King Polixenes was outraged that his son should become engaged to a shepherd's daughter – and without his permission! He threw off his hat and false beard and angrily forbade the engagement. "Thou art too base to be acknowledg'd," he cried to his son. "Follow us to the court."

But Camillo was charmed by the two young lovers and thought he might use their love to his advantage. As soon as King Polixenes was out of earshot, he persuaded them to escape to Sicily and beg King Leontes' support for their marriage. He felt sure that Leontes would not refuse to help the son of his old friend Polixenes. "Methinks I see Leontes opening his free arms and weeping his welcomes forth," he assured them.

Camillo hoped that once Florizel and Perdita were safely aboard a ship to Sicily, he would be able to bring Polixenes around to the idea of the marriage and follow the pair back to his beloved homeland.

So the two lovers travelled to Sicily, accompanied by the shepherd. As Camillo had predicted, King Leontes welcomed Prince Florizel to his court with open arms, crying, "Most dearly welcome! And your fair princess – goddess!"

Leontes could not stop staring at Perdita – she looked exactly like his lost wife. Sad memories came flooding back to him, and he told his guests how he had caused the deaths of his wife and son and sent his daughter away.

As King Leontes talked, it dawned on the shepherd that Perdita could be Leontes' daughter. At first no one could believe this possible, but finally all agreed it must be so.

Many rumours flew about the court as to how it was proved. One gentleman swore the baby was found with the mantle of Queen Hermione. "Methought I heard the shepherd say he found the child," whispered another.

Leontes was overcome with happiness. "The Oracle is fulfilled," everyone agreed.

Perdita wanted to know what her mother had looked like, so Paulina agreed to show her a statue of the queen, which she kept at her house. When she drew the curtain from around the statue, the princess and her father gasped – Hermione looked so lifelike, and so very like Perdita.

"Chide me, dear stone, that I may say indeed thou art Hermione," the king whispered in wonder. "The very life seems warm upon her lip."

He could not take his eyes off the statue. The sculptor must have been most talented, he thought, for this statue showed Hermione as she might have looked that very day, older than when husband and wife had last met. "Hermione was not so much wrinkled," he remarked.

Paulina smiled and called for music. To everyone's amazement, the statue began to move. Slowly, as though waking from a long dream, Hermione – for it was really her – descended the pedestal and embraced Leontes.

"O, she's warm!" he sighed, "If this be magic, let it be an art lawful as eating."

Hermione had always kept faith in the Oracle. Believing that one day Perdita would be found, she waited in secret, walking like a ghost through the castle, hoping for this moment. Now, after so many years of loneliness, she was reunited with both her husband and her daughter.

When King Polixenes arrived and discovered his son's shepherdess was actually a princess, he gave his blessing for Florizel and Perdita's marriage. So the two families were joined in harmony once more.

Only Paulina, who had helped bring about this happiness, was dissatisfied, for her husband had never returned from his encounter with the bear on the shores of Bohemia.

"I, an old turtle, will wing me to some wither'd bough and there my mate, that's never to be found again, lament till I am lost," she grumped.

"O, peace, Paulina!" laughed Leontes. "Thou shouldst a husband take. Come, Camillo…"

He gave Paulina's hand in marriage to Camillo, for they had long held each other in deep affection.

So ended the strange story of how Paulina kept Hermione hidden and how Perdita was found – a wonderful winter's tale to tell by the fireside. For although the tale is tinged with sadness, as poor Prince Mamillius once said, "A sad tale's best for winter."

THE END

Marcia Williams

With her distinctive cartoon-strip style, lively text and brilliant wit, Marcia Williams brings to life some of the world's all-time favourite stories and some colourful historical characters. Her hilarious retellings and clever observations will have children laughing out loud and coming back for more!

ISBN 978-1-4063-3832-4   ISBN 978-1-4063-4492-9   ISBN 978-1-4063-2610-9   ISBN 978-1-4063-1944-6

ISBN 978-1-4063-2334-4   ISBN 978-1-4063-2335-1   ISBN 978-1-4063-0563-0   ISBN 978-1-4063-0562-3

ISBN 978-1-4063-1137-2   ISBN 978-1-4063-1866-1   ISBN 978-1-4063-0348-3   ISBN 978-1-4063-3199-8

ISBN 978-1-4063-4694-7   ISBN 978-1-4063-5455-3   ISBN 978-1-4063-5316-7   ISBN 978-1-4063-5268-9

Available from all good booksellers

www.walker.co.uk